NOT FORGOTTEN

ELIZABETH JOHNS

BRETHREN IN ARMS PROLOGUE

Vitoria, Northern Spain, June 1813
The Allied Encampment

*T*he grief was so thick in their throats, none could speak. They had been together for only two years, yet the bonds of the battle were forged stronger than any created by blood. It was not something that could be explained, only experienced.

When they had set sail from England for the Peninsula, each had felt invincible, ready to conquer evil and save England. Now, it was hard to remember why they needed to be brave any more.

There was a chill in the air as they all sat huddled around the fire. James shivered. The silence the night before a battle was eerie, but afterwards, it was deafening. Watching the campfire's flames perform their blue, gold and orange dance, it did not seem real that one of them was gone. They had survived Ciudad Rodrigo, Badajoz, and Salamanca, yet Peter had fallen before their eyes today. His sabre had been raised and his eyes fierce, ready to charge when a shot had seared through him. He was on his horse one moment and gone the next. The scene replayed over and over in their minds in slow-motion. Memory was a cruel, cruel master. The same battle had left Luke wounded when a shell exploded near him. He had insisted on joining them tonight, eschewing the orders of the sawbones and hobbling out of the medical tent on the arm of his batman, Tobin.

Now, there were six of them left, if Peter's widow was included, and all wondered, *Was this to be their fate?*

Someone had to speak and break the chain of their morbid, damning thoughts.

"Peter would not want this." Four pairs of morose eyes looked up at Matthias. "We all knew this was likely when we signed up to fight Napoleon."

"How would you want us to feel if it were you?" James asked.

"I would want you to keep going and give my life meaning."

"Precisely. We mourn this night and move forward tomorrow. His death shall not be in vain," James said with quiet conviction.

"I still do not understand how we were caught unawares. Unless…" Colin was replaying the scene over in his mind.

"Someone gave our position away." Luke voiced what they all suspected.

"We were ambushed," Matthias added. In the end, England had emerged the victor, but it had been a near thing.

"What about Kitty?" Peter's wife followed the drum and felt like one of them.

"We see what she wishes to do. I expect she will wish to return home," Matthias answered. He had known her and Peter from the cradle and was the most devastated by the loss.

"The French are worn down; this cannot go on much longer," Luke said, though he would be sent home. No one else dared voice such hope.

"We are worn down," James muttered.

Philip, the quiet, thoughtful one, spoke. "If anything happens to me, will someone look to my sister? She has no one else."

"I swear it," Colin said, leading the others to do the same.

"Pietas et honos."

Philip nodded, too affected to speak.

"Loyalty and honour." Another swore the oath in English.

They returned to silence, each brooding over what had happened and what was yet to come.

CHAPTER 1

Spring 1814

"Kill them all if they are not already dead," a distant female voice said in French.

Philip felt as though he were dreaming and struggled to pay attention. He wanted to go to sleep, but years of military training was telling his instincts that he had better be on alert. Where was he? He tried to remember. There was sand beneath his cheek and he felt very, very wet. Remaining as still as possible, he attempted to look through his lashes; there was a thud nearby and a spray of sand splattered him. He fought to maintain absolute stillness.

"It is a pity," the female voice said again, much nearer this time. "He was an excellent source of information, but could no longer be trusted."

Philip knew that voice, but he could not place it at the moment.

"Hawthorne was your puppet," a male voice spat, "and had become a liability."

"*Oui*, but a very useful one." She sighed. "It had to be done."

"Not a moment too soon," the man grunted. "He did not approve of our plans and would have eventually betrayed us."

"Perhaps. Has there been any sign of the Englishman?" she asked.

The hairs stood on the back of Philip's head. He was an Englishman.

"*Non.* He could not have survived the blast. He will eventually be washed ashore."

"I suppose you are correct. Take care of the bodies. I will send news of their deaths to the Duke."

"Which Duke?" the henchman asked.

"Both, I suppose. Wellington and I understand each other. Captain Elliot was one of his favourites, and Waverley is my niece's husband. I owe them that, I suppose."

"Very good, Madame."

After he thought they had gone, Philip waited a few more minutes before moving. He looked around slowly, then stood, taking stock of the scene around him. He was hidden behind an outcrop of rocks, which was why he had not been seen. The unfortunates on the ship had apparently been washed up on the shore not far from where they had set sail. Remnants of a boat lay scattered along the sand and floated in the water. Dead bodies had been spat out of the great deep, including that of Hawthorne—the English prisoner and traitor Philip had been escorting to the West Indies, after which he was supposed to go on to America to help with the war there.

"Cursed luck," he muttered as he knelt down to ensure the man was dead. The man's eyes stared lifelessly at the sky, and no heartbeat could be felt at his fleshy neck. Scars marked his body, presumably from the splintering of the wood, and he was already growing cold and bloated from being drowned.

Looking at the wreck, Philip could understand why they assumed no one had survived. Clearly, he needed to find shelter and hide. Quickly searching the pockets of the nearby bodies, he found a few items that might come in handy later—Hawthorne's watch, a knife, a few coins and wet paper bills. Then he took some water and erased any signs of his presence before following the tracks the others had made in the sand. Hopefully the workers brought back to deal with the bodies would not realize he had been there.

He returned to the outcrop in the rocky cliff to hide and be protected from the elements. Crouching down, he waited, hoping to gather more information about who he had heard on the beach. At first glance, it appeared a storm could have done this, but the couple had spoken as if they had taken care of Hawthorne deliberately. *He could not have survived the blast.*

What should he do next? Somehow he would need to get word to Wellington, but first, he needed to know who these people were and exactly what had happened.

The sun was beginning to lower in the evening sky, and Philip wondered if the men would return before morning. He wanted to remove his wet boots and clothing, but did not dare leave himself exposed and vulnerable until he had more information.

He seemed to be intact, he thought, surveying himself. There were no serious wounds that he could discern and no pain worth the mention. Although he felt exhausted, and could not remember any details of the shipwreck, he did recall Hawthorne and his mission, so that was something, at least. They must still be in France, since the woman and her companion had spoken in the language. The coast looked similar to where they had set sail, with a small beach and rocky cliffs.

After more than an hour by the sun's movement, a few men returned in boats and collected the bodies. Philip frowned. He was certain there was something important about that.

It was difficult to make out much of what they were saying as they gathered up remains and loaded them into the dinghies. One man looked around in confusion. He was tall and dark with an air of command. Philip assumed he was the man who had been there before with the woman and then realized something was wrong. The man shook his head as though he had imagined something. No doubt they were to bury the bodies in the water, and never mention it again.

"Madame Lisette will not be pleased," the man said to himself before walking to the boat and climbing in.

Madame Lisette. La Glacier.

Everything began to make sense. Philip knew he recognized the voice he had heard before. The man looked around one more time and threw up his hands, yet whatever concerned him was not enough to delay their departure. The boats pushed off from the shore and rowed away around the cliff's edge.

As the sun began to set, Philip removed his boots and decided to rest for a couple of hours. Then he could decide what to do with a clear head. One thing he knew, he wanted nothing to do with Napoleon's mistress. She was as conniving as she was beautiful, and probably did have ice running through her veins. Philip distrusted her completely. However, she was the Emperor's confidant, and he should probably do his best to learn her secrets.

There was nothing else to do but establish himself here and try to discover the plan, but it would be best if *La Glacier* never discovered he was alive.

He was a master of disguise, but so was she. Would she recognize him? They had interacted closely when negotiating Tobin's release. A woman who survived on her beauty and wits never forgot a detail. She had made no secret that she was attracted to him, but could he use that to his advantage? Sometimes it was a necessary evil. Remembering Hawthorne's dead body, he cringed, even though the man had deserved a much harsher death for his treason. Philip had to find a way to discover the plans mentioned. She would not hesitate to kill him if she discovered he was alive and attempting to spy on her. Philip shuddered as an idea began to form in his mind.

He surveyed his wounds as he removed his wet clothing and stockings. A few substantial gashes were the worst, so he cleaned and bandaged them as best he could, then he settled down for an uncomfortable sleep amongst the rocks, to the sounds of the waves that hours before had almost killed him.

Late Autumn 1814

LADY AMELIA BLAKE watched the dancers across the overly warm, crowded ballroom as she sipped her lemonade. It was a brief reprieve. Finding a moment alone was something to be cherished. Her first London Season had been as grand as she had imagined, and she had more suitors than she could count. She had been a glorious success by all accounts. However, London had been one thing which she had not imagined—suffocating. Her time was not her own, and she felt smothered. There had been many offers for her hand, but none of them was the one she wanted. Now they had moved into autumn and she could not wait to get away from the crush and into the country.

"Why the long face, sister?"

Amelia sighed. Her sister had made a love-match with a duke and was deliriously happy. How could Amelia tell Meg what she really thought?

"I am tired. Town is fatiguing."

"I thought you were indefatigable. You have more élan than anyone I know," the Duchess said with a sceptical look, those pale eyes boring into her.

"Alas, I am human after all."

"Are you any closer to choosing a suitor? Ashford, Wadsworth, and Blankenstyn are all waiting for answers. Perhaps once you decide, you will feel some relief."

"I do not think I can, Meg," Amelia said softly. Her sister directed her out to the terrace which was of grey stone and guarded by marble statues devoid of heads.

"You cannot wait for him, Amelia," Meg whispered with determinedness. "We do not know where he is or what he is doing. He made you no promises in the five minutes in which you were acquainted with him," Meg said harshly. "I am sorry to be so frank, but you are leading all these gentlemen to believe they have a chance of securing your affections when you have no intention of accepting them, and for what? A girlhood infatuation!"

Amelia crossed her arms and turned away. What her sister said was true. Captain Elliot had made her no promises, but he had made her heart sing. No one else had come close to affecting her the way he had.

"What you say is true," she admitted, "but in good conscience, I cannot accept any of my current suitors."

"Then you had best refuse them all and stop deceiving them. Your reputation will not survive playing fast and loose for long, my sister."

"I do not mean to play with their affections. I thought to flirt and laugh and pray one of them would touch my heart."

Amelia could see the disappointment on Meg's face and her eyes pitied her. "You have made no false promises?"

"No, none. I would not do such a thing!"

"Perhaps you have been *burning the midnight oil*, as Luke would say. Some time in the country might do you good."

"That will start vicious rumours," Amelia warned.

"Not if we blame it on my condition," her sister said as her fingers travelled over the slight bulge in her stomach.

"I suppose not, but will it make any difference?" Amelia threw up her hands.

"I cannot answer that for you."

Meg directed Amelia to a stone bench down the steps in the garden and farther from the crowds. It was a cool evening and neither had a shawl to cover their shoulders from the chill breeze.

"Sister, there has already been much talk. You must forget Captain Elliot. No one has heard from him since that cryptic message Luke received at Adelaide's wedding. We do not know when it was sent, nor from where. I am sure he would have made an appearance by now if he were alive."

Amelia blew out a breath of frustration and sadness. Looking down at her hands, she swallowed hard.

"I know what you say is true. I know it is not realistic to pine for Captain Elliot, but I want someone to make me feel the way he did. I do not know what I am hoping for." She shook her head to fight tears. Meg put her arm around her and gave her a hug.

"I am sorry, Amelia. Finding a mate is hard, especially when you hope for more than an alliance. There are some very good men wishing for your hand. Are none of them a possibility? What about Captain Frome? You are always smiling and laughing with him. You could do much worse than someone you have fun with."

She looked to the captain, who cut a dashing figure in his dark blue uniform which set off his ginger curls to perfection. His dimpled smile and unruly charm had undoubtedly reduced many a fashionable miss to sighing and dreaming...not unlike another captain she could think of.

"For one, he is the last person to want to settle down. He has made that clear. For two, he is easy for me to be myself with because he feels like a brother. He does not take anything seriously and who would want to marry someone like that?"

"I think there is much more to him than he reveals. Come, it is growing cold." They stood and walked back to the terrace. "I will speak to Waverley about retiring to the country early before Christmastide. I think a holiday would benefit all of us."

"Very well," Amelia said in resignation.

Meg kissed Amelia on the cheek before returning to the ballroom. Amelia watched through the windows as her sister went back inside to the Duke. He was the tall and dark contrast to her small, light beauty. He greeted her with love in his eyes and Amelia felt a pang of jealousy. How desperately she wanted what they had.

"Is that too much to ask for?" She looked toward the stars in the sky for an answer.

"Whatever you are asking for, I will gladly give you," a voice whispered into her neck, sending shivers up her spine. If she closed her eyes, she could pretend it was Captain Elliot coming to rescue her from this whirlwind of madness she had been caught up in. Instead, it was Lord Wadsworth, trying to catch her in a compromising position.

Amelia jumped back towards the door. "Lord Wadsworth! You should not sneak up on people," she said, lifting her hand to her chest.

"That was not the response I was hoping for," he murmured seductively, stepping close enough that she could see his blond whiskers move with his breath.

"Sir, forgive me. I feel a headache coming on. I should seek my sister and return home."

Considering the suspicious smirk he gave her, he obviously saw right through her falsehood. However, he graciously offered her his arm.

"Then I will return you to the Duchess." She could do nothing but accept.

He said nothing as they walked across the ballroom to her sister, but he looked around the room and nodded to people as they passed by. His figure was fine, though tailored to an inch of his life, but it did not explain the stares. Amelia had been in London long enough to realize people were beginning to whisper about them. When they reached the Duke and Duchess, Waverley stepped forward and held out his hand to Wadsworth.

"What is happening?" Meg asked.

"Why, my dear, Wadsworth went out to the terrace to ask Amelia for her hand. I assume by the smile on his face that congratulations are in order."

Amelia let out a gasp and cast a withering look at Lord Wadsworth.

"I will call on you in the morning, sir. Lady Amelia has a headache and would like to return home."

For the first time in her life, Amelia was speechless. Before she could object, Lord Wadsworth was walking away to receive congratulations from those people within hearing of the conversation. The news would spread like fire before they even left the ball.

Meg whispered in her ear, "I did not think you would come to your senses so quickly."

"I did no such thing!" she said objected through gritted teeth. "Please take me home before I commit a murder and am thrown in the Tower."

"Oh, dear," Meg said, looking at the Duke, who was frowning. He glared at Wadsworth and then escorted them out to the carriage which was outside along the street.

"This is a very serious matter," he said to Amelia as he handed them inside.

"Are you not coming with us?" Meg asked her husband.

"No. I want to stay and witness what words are being spread. I do not want to take any action until the morning. Amelia, you know we will not force you to marry anyone, but there will be consequences if you decide not to marry him."

"I do not care what is said, so long as I am not forced to marry such a lying, deceitful, cheat!" She looked away before she burst into tears. She had been so careful, and to fall prey to this rogue in a moment of weakness was too much for her sensibilities.

"Promise you will not call him out," Meg begged as Waverley closed the door and told the driver to take them home.

CHAPTER 2

*P*hilip ducked into an alleyway when he saw the familiar face. It had been months since he had seen someone he recognized. He knew Waverley's man, Tobin, had been searching for him, and he had almost found him. Pangs of guilt washed over Philip as he thought of his sister and the trials he must have put her through. Their parents having died, each other was all they had left. He had told Wellington where he was, of course, but the danger was too great for his sister, Adelaide, to know where he was.

Had they not received his message that he was alive? He watched Tobin go into an inn across the narrow cobblestone near the open market. He would know those green eyes and black hair anywhere.

"Why the devil is he here?" Philip whispered under his breath. "I am too close now for this to fail."

"*Monsieur*! I have the delivery ready for the fortress."

"*Oui*. I am ready," he called back.

It had taken him months of living in this small village outside La Glacier's stronghold to gain access to the fortress, a castle-like manor home sitting atop the great chalk cliffs of Étretat, which disguised a network of rooms, tunnels, cells and caves for Napoleon's empire. It had been even longer before he became a confidant of those working for La Glacier. Something important was about to happen—Philip could feel it in his bones. He needed to discover what it was before it happened.

He loaded his cart with candles, oil and flour, and set the old chestnut horses on the path up the steep slope. As he drove, he allowed himself to think of England a little. He could not dwell too long, for homesickness would weaken his senses, but he was so tired of being in disguise and living the life of a peasant when his heart was in England. "It is England you are doing this for, *un jeu d'enfant*," he chastised himself.

Pulling up to the gates of the heavily guarded fortress, he saw they were already opened.

"What is this?" he asked. No guards were in sight, but he knew them to be there.

The last thing he wanted was to be seen by La Glacier. His disguise would not hold water with her for a moment. He pulled the cart around into some trees and watched. A few minutes passed before he heard the clatter of horses' hoofs and then he saw them pull through the gate, drawing a white travelling carriage behind them. Quickly the conveyance picked up speed and for a moment Philip debated following, but his two elderly job horses would never keep up, and the risk of being caught was too great. With a curse and a frown, he drove his old nags through the gate and went around to the kitchen. Hopefully, for a little flirtation, one of the maids would have some information again.

"*Bonjour, Monsieur,*" a buxom maid said as he stood at the door to the kitchen. "I have been waiting for you."

"Bonjour, Josefina. Have you had visitors? A carriage almost ran over me when leaving the gates."

"*Non.* The mistress is on her way to Paris."

"Does she go there often?"

"*Oui.* Whenever she needs a new hat." Josefina winked.

"I would like to buy you a new hat when I become a rich man," he said flirtatiously, moving a little closer.

"And when will that be, hmm? I might be willing to give more than my kisses for a promise."

"Sadly, my promises would be empty... unless I could free the Emperor and gain his favours." He tried to look dejected.

"That is what my mistress is working for. Even now, on her way to Paris, they are scheming," she whispered.

"Josefina! The eggs will not gather themselves!" the Cook scolded as she came back into the room. "If they start walking in here, you will have to pluck them all by yourself."

Josefina giggled and planted a kiss on Philip's lips. "Until later, *Monsieur*. Wednesday is my half-day."

"I will see you in the village then," he called as she ran back to her duties.

It was as he suspected; there was a plot to free Napoleon. But how? And when?

He unloaded his cart and continued around to the stables. He had become friendly with some of the grooms, and he liked to admire the horses. He missed his own trusty steed, Scipio, who had saved him time and again in battle. He was now housed with Wellington's cattle, and he longed to be reunited with him.

No one noticed Philip, so intent were they on their tasks. Philip left the cart and horses near a grassy area where they could graze, and crept around to observe.

"They are preparing for a long trip," he observed, feeling his frown deepen.

Footsteps crunched in the pebbled drive, so Philip moved casually away from his spying post into the stable yard.

"*Monsieur Lefebre*! 'Ave you come to admire the horses again?" a groom asked as he put down a pail of water he was carrying.

"But of course. How else will I ever come close to such beauty?" He followed the plump, jovial groom into the stable.

"I suspect you have your fair share of *les amoureux*, but none compares to the horse, *oui*?"

"*Non*. A horse does not betray its master like the fickle ladies." Philip picked up a brush and began to rub down the horse.

The groom looked at him with sympathy and they brushed down the white mare—all of La Glacier's horses were white—in comfortable silence. When the mare had been given her oats, Philip nodded towards the barn outside. "Expecting a harsh winter? I noticed the extra stores being placed in the barn, and I had more orders than usual."

"The mistress." The man waved his hand flamboyantly as if it explained everything.

Philip grunted knowingly.

"She goes to visit the Emperor soon. We were told to be ready when she returns from Paris."

"Ah, lovesickness. Perhaps she will stay with him." Philip chuckled.

"*Non.* She has gone before and always returns."

"I need a woman who knows when to leave!"

The men laughed and shared a pint of ale and Philip left without asking more. It would not do to make them suspicious. It had taken months for the groom to confide that much.

He left feeling a new sense of purpose. There had been an undercurrent of energy running through the fortress. Something was about to happen. He had to let Wellington know and consider how he was to stop whatever La Glacier had planned.

On his return to the village, having stabled his horses and locked up his cart, he hurried to his rooms. They were far nicer than they should have been for his meagre occupation, but he had spent enough time in the trenches whilst at war.

The two small rooms were in the attics of a widowed lady's home. He helped her with some of the heavy tasks around the house, and she kept him in good food.

He sat at his small writing desk and pulled out a piece of paper to write to Wellington.

"I can deliver that for ye," a deep Irish brogue said from behind him. Philip jumped to his feet and turned in one, swift movement, his knife unsheathed.

"How the devil did you get in here?"

"I walked in, *mo charid*," Tobin said with a smirk.

Philip let out the breath he was holding and threw his knife on the desk. "How did you find me?"

"Wellington sent me."

Philip slumped down into his chair and glared at Tobin while he waited for the explanation.

"Well?" he demanded at last.

"Ye have led me a merry dance for the past few months. Not to mention yer sister, and all of yer comrades. Oh, I danced with yer sister at her wedding. She looked beautiful, by the way."

That hurt deeply, as Tobin no doubt intended, but he would not let this rascal know how much. So Adelaide had married. At least she had someone else to protect her.

"Who did she marry?"

"Major Fielding."

Philip whistled. He supposed if anyone could have leg-shackled Fielding it would have to have been his sister, and he could think of no finer man for Adelaide.

"You have been in the military long enough to know that secrecy is a necessary evil, Tobin. Are you going to tell me why Wellington compromised my position and sent you here?"

"Don't be daft. I did not compromise anything."

"Is that why I saw you walking through the village this morning?"

Tobin scoffed. "I am trying to decide whether to darken your daylights before I tell you why I am here."

"You are welcome to try," Philip retorted, and raised a haughty eyebrow. "I have plenty of spleen I could expend on you."

"That will do neither of us any good jus' now," Tobin said wisely.

"So what message does our commander have for me?" Philip held out his hand for the usual coded message.

Tobin shook his head. "He did not wish to put it in writing."

Philip narrowed his eyes but waited.

"La Glacier has gone to Paris as you likely know."

Philip inclined his head.

"Wellington wants to know what her meeting is about."

"She would know me in a heartbeat. That is what has made this assignment so difficult. I can only get information from servants."

"Wellington also requested Waverley to bring the Duchess and her sister to visit their aunt. He expects them within a week."

Phillip's heart sped up. A beautiful redhead with a brilliant smile flashed through his memories.

"I see you have not forgotten the Lady Amelia," Tobin said knowingly.

Philip picked up his knife and tossed it at Tobin's head, hitting only a few inches away for fun.

Tobin held up his hands. "No need to become possessive. She is yours if you can catch her."

Philip crossed his arms and glared, ignoring Tobin's insolence. "What does Wellington want me to do?"

"Resume your position as the dashing Captain Elliot and join their party."

"The servants will recognize me."

"Ye've a good disguise. When back in yer fancy toff's dress and clean shaven, speaking the King's English, no one will know."

"I suppose I should go to Paris, then, and refresh my wardrobe?"

"That is why I've come. Make a big fuss about leaving town and we will depart in the morning. You will return with the party from Paris after the meeting."

"Waverley knows?"

"And Major and Mrs. Fielding."

"My sister will be there?" he asked, but daring to hope.

"We couldna keep her away."

Philip smiled. "I will be ready."

AMELIA AND MEG SAT UP, waiting for the Duke to return. They had exhausted all the possibilities of what to do, but now, mostly Amelia wanted to go to bed and wake up to find the whole evening had been just a nightmare.

"We were so close to leaving Town," Meg opined. "How could this have happened?"

"Wadsworth is under the hatches. He was desperate," the Duke answered from the doorway.

"I did not hear you come in!" Meg said, looking at her husband.

"So you have nothing good to report," Amelia declared. "Then I am going to bed."

"I think you should stay," Waverley said. "I have had some news."

Amelia sat back down in her chair in Meg's sitting room. Rarely did Waverley ask or command her to do anything, thankfully. He went to pour himself a drink, which only served to increase the suspense she felt.

When he had loosened his neckcloth and was sitting in his favourite chair by the hearth, he finally spoke.

"I have had a letter from Wellington."

Meg looked as though she would cry. "I do not understand," she said. "What does he want?"

"He has asked us to go to France. All of us...to visit your aunt."

Both ladies looked at him blankly. They had barely spoken of their aunt since the incident where Amelia had been kidnapped and the Duke's man, Tobin, had rescued her. Tobin had been taken captive and the Duke and her sister had rescued him. That had been when Captain Elliot had gone missing. Amelia preferred to not think of those horrible events. Her aunt, whom she had not known existed, was the famous La Glacier—one of Napoleon's ex-mistresses—and her uncle Hawthorne had been committing treason against England by consorting with her. Amelia could not help being intrigued by this aunt but had not been allowed to communicate with or see her.

"Why would Wellington want that?" Meg asked.

"She has been having meetings. It seems she is carrying on with Napoleon's work in his absence. There are rumblings of an uprising. There is also a meeting in Paris next week."

"He wants us to spy on our aunt?" Amelia asked. "How very singular!"

"You do not need to do anything," Waverley said to his wife.

"I do not want either of you in danger, especially not in your condition, my love."

"She would not hurt us," Meg protested.

"I think you underestimate her, especially if she was aware you had betrayed her," Waverley retorted. "She ordered Hawthorne's ship to go down."

Amelia and Meg both let out a gasp. Meg covered her mouth with her hands. "I cannot believe it of her!"

"Perhaps she cares more for her own flesh and blood, but she is ruthless for her cause nonetheless. Hawthorne deserved his death, but other, innocent people did not."

Amelia could not keep from thinking of Captain Elliot, whom she had not seen since that whole incident.

"I would like to go. Why not take me and leave Meg behind in safety?"

"Absolutely not!" Meg protested. "She is my aunt, as well. If we can do something to right the wrongs committed by our family, we should go."

Waverley looked hesitant.

"I will not let you leave me behind," Meg insisted in a firm voice that she rarely used with the Duke.

Amelia sat back and waited for him to object.

"You know very well I can refuse you nothing. However, you must promise me you will be extremely careful. Do not let her fool you because she is your aunt."

"I promise. I still remember that day." Meg made a face of disgust.

"She did return Tobin to us, and I have not forgotten that," he conceded.

"Hopefully, she is doing nothing wrong and we can have a pleasant visit with family," Amelia added sardonically.

Waverley scoffed at her comment. "If hell has frozen." He leaned over his chair and kissed his wife on the cheek. "It is late. We must be up early in the morning."

"But the servants will have to spend all night packing!"

"Unfortunately, yes, but duty calls. We pay them well for such service, my dear." He assisted her out of her chair, and they started across the room to retire.

"Wait!" Amelia demanded. "What about Wadsworth? Are we just to leave Town and allow rumours to swirl?"

"I took care of him." Pausing with Meg's hand on his arm, the Duke spoke with a wave of his other hand before once more turning to leave.

How nice it must be for him to hold such power, Amelia thought. "Do not leave me in suspense!" she cried.

Waverley turned back again with a harsh look on his face which softened when he saw her pleas.

"Forgive me, I am tired. He was willing to back away from his claims for a financial incentive."

"He gets away with his misconduct so easily?" she asked, realizing she sounded ungrateful.

"You know me better than that. I have put it about in the clubs, what really happened. He will have to leave Town for some time."

"And my good name?"

"Is still intact. We are leaving for Paris on a holiday. I ordered you to leave and recover and consider your future."

"I suppose it is the best I could hope for, all things considered. Thank you for coming to my rescue. I only hope it did not cost my entire dowry to reward him for his deplorable behaviour."

"I doubt he considers my purchasing all of his vowels, and giving him a loan, a reward. Good night."

Amelia could not prevent a smile as he walked out of the room. Her sister had married a good man. "And a knowing one at that," she murmured as she took herself to bed for the night. Exhaustion should have caused her to sleep, but there was too much on her mind when she climbed into bed. It hurt deeply that Wadsworth would stoop to such measures. She had thought them friends, but she had not encouraged him, either. Had she known his desperation, she would have been more careful.

Through the hurt, she could not help but feel a little anticipation and excitement at going to France. She would finally meet her elusive aunt and perhaps try her hand at spying. She had always longed for more activity than was allowed to gently bred females, and the excitement that gentlemen were able to experience. Captain Elliot has had an adventurous life in the army, she thought, "and, indeed, it might have got him killed," she reminded herself aloud. Was he dead or alive? Would being in France allow her to search for him?

She did not know why she thought she could find him when especially trained investigators had not been able to do so, but her heart longed to find him. Would he even remember her? He could have been injured, or could be imprisoned. She turned over and beat her pillow with her fist in frustration.

"Why can I not be content with one of my suitors?" she demanded of its linen-covered softness. Nevertheless, she was glad to have discovered Wadsworth's true colours before they had married. She was fortunate to have a duke to protect her, otherwise she would have been forced to accept the marriage to save her reputation.

Grateful for a reprieve from the Season, Amelia allowed herself to dream of Paris. Never having been fortunate enough to leave England, she had heard stories of Paris's beauty and fashion. Now that Bonaparte was in exile, and under the support of Wellington, they could have a taste of such pleasures. Frenchmen had never been to her taste, but to be fair, she had not met very many. Perhaps they would be surrounded by Wellington's finest and someone could help her forget Captain Elliot. Truly, she needed—no, wanted—to forget him. Meg was right, she was hanging on to a girlhood infatuation and measuring everyone else against him. He had given no indication that he harboured any thought of thinking of her again. London was full of young bucks just like him: a handsome face coupled with outrageous flirtations. Why was he different to her? She could not answer that with any satisfaction, but she did finally fall asleep with a smile on her face, to dream of him.

CHAPTER 3

"What are ye doing, ye ejeet?" Tobin asked with such seriousness that Philip had to laugh.

"Since when do you call a superior officer an idiot?" Philip asked sternly.

"Give me thirty lashes, sir. I have not learned to control my tongue. Likely, I never will."

"Remember who rescued you, Tobin. We will say no more about it. Save your 'idiots' for the Duke if he tolerates such insolence," Philip quipped. "I am staying in my peasants' garb until we reach Paris. It will make travelling easier."

"Will it? Ye do not think people will question why ye are dressed like that on one of Wellington's fine horses?"

"I am not riding his horse," Philip answered, unperturbed. "Let us not delay. The meeting is in a few days, and there is much to do."

"*Gombeen*." However, Tobin took one of Philip's small satchels of belongings and followed his superior to the stables. "Ye are taking the old cart?" Tobin asked once he saw Philip's intentions as he had the old nags hooked to the aged conveyance.

"Yes. I will explain once we are out of the village. Go on ahead and wait for me at the stream where the road forks."

Philip kept Tobin waiting two hours. He knew the Irishman would be fuming, and pacing the leather from his boots with impatience, but the time lost selling the cart and horses to a farmer outside the village would gain them in the long run.

Having arrived at the meeting point and been treated to a surly reception, he changed his clothing in the bushes and mounted one of the horses, a big grin spreading over Philip's face.

"Once I shave, hopefully no one will recognize me, but since we are returning here later, I wanted to make certain people would not be suspicious. Now, let us move on; we have no time to lose if we are to make it in time for the meeting," Philip directed, receiving, in response, some murderous Irish curse laced heavily with sarcasm.

The pair arrived in Paris after two days of hard riding, in which they carefully avoided the main roads where they might be recognized. Philip could not but feel relieved once they arrived at Wellington's headquarters in Paris. It would be nice to be himself again, he thought—if only briefly.

"Captain Elliot!" Wellington boomed from the balcony above their heads before Tobin and Philip had even handed their hats to the butler. "I saw you ride in. It is about time."

Phillip glared at Tobin, daring him to speak on why they had been delayed.

"Come on up," the Duke called.

Philip and Tobin made their way to the Duke's office, a high-ceilinged white room with tall double doors on three sides, and windows looking out over the gardens on the other. A large table filled the centre of the room, covered with papers and maps, and officers pouring over them.

Wellington, dressed trimly in his customary plain monochrome suit and shortly cropped hair, greeted Philip formally. "It will be nice to have you in the land of the living again, Captain Elliot, even if you do look like a hermit who has never seen a razor. It is not pleasant to look your sister in the eye and lie to her, but duty comes first."

"I did not imagine it was easy to conceal the truth from her."

"Fortunately, you can do the explaining to her later. First, allow me to acquaint you with the situation with La Glacier *nee* Madame Lisette."

"First, sir, are you aware she is planning to visit Elba? I was at the fortress a few days ago, and they were preparing for a voyage," Philip explained.

"No, I was not aware, but it does not surprise me." Finger and thumb to his mouth, Wellington started thinking, as he tended to do. Both soldiers knew better than to speak.

"I should send word to Elba. My sources tell me he is comfortable there, ruling the place. It would not surprise me if he quit the island from under their very noses. Is there anyone you can trust at the fortress to inform you when they set sail?"

"Unfortunately, I have but lately become well enough acquainted with some of the servants. It was very difficult, at first, to even enter the fortress."

"The servants do right to be suspicious. Most urgent is the meeting that is to take place on the morrow. It is being held at her house on the Rue Cambon. I have placed people in the vicinity, at the taverns and brothels, but I was only able to get one person inside the kitchens."

"I could make the attempt as *Monsieur Lefebre*," Philip offered.

Wellington shook his head. "It is too dangerous, given your previous associations. She is no fool and it will do no good to arouse her suspicions from the start. If she did not, one of her men would be bound to recognize you. Besides, I need you to be a part of Waverley's party."

"I do not understand, sir. I do not think La Glacier is likely to let down her guard if I am around."

"She might if you are wooing her niece."

"So that is what this is about... the incomparable Lady Amelia." Philip stood up and began to pace restlessly about the room. "How was that arranged? I cannot imagine her willingly leaving London Society."

"Things have been arranged. I expect them any day now."

Philip stopped and turned towards the Duke. "Sir, I think my talents would be better spent trying to discover from the meeting what her plans are."

"You underestimate your appeal, Elliot. You may have two days to discover what you can about the meeting, but after that your attention goes to Lady Amelia...or La Glacier, if the wind is blowing in that direction." He winked at Philip.

"Is Waverley amenable to this plan? Because I could see myself married or dead if he is not.... and more likely the latter, now I come to think on it. I am not certain he would consider me acceptable for his sister."

"He has some idea. I will speak with him, though. Worry not."

"Lady Amelia is the one you should be worried about." Tobin spoke for the first time.

"Is the threat so great that we must bring Lady Amelia in? Is she acting in an official capacity, as a spy?"

"The Duchess and Lady Amelia are to be just what they are—Madame Lisette's nieces. She will be rightly suspicious of you and Waverley."

"Ah, so I am a decoy?"

"We are hoping to force her into making a mistake. An element of surprise, if you will."

Philip doubted the lady did anything by mistake, but he did not say so.

"When do we leave Paris?"

"I have no control with regards to the lady. She may choose to welcome her family here instead of returning to her fortress."

"There is good and bad to either choice."

"True enough, but I know you two and Waverley are up to the task."

"Two?" Tobin and Philip asked simultaneously.

"It makes perfect sense to have you there as well, Tobin, being formerly the Duke's man. The more eyes and ears, the better. You are welcome to stay here. I have been invited to a party at her *hôtel* tomorrow evening and you will attend with me. Otherwise, I want a report every morning you are in Paris," Wellington remarked, dismissing them with a gesture of his hand.

"Yes, sir." Philip and Tobin stood and saluted their Commander. Turning away, they left in silence.

They were shown to their rooms, in a different wing of the residence, by a smartly liveried servant. Then they began to plan how they would try to gain information about the meeting.

"She would recognize both of us in a heartbeat," Tobin said as they sat down in the comfortable blue arm chairs flanking the marble fireplace in Philip's rooms.

On a piece of paper he found in a drawer, Philip began to sketch out the area surrounding La Glacier's house and the alleyways surrounding it.

"Fortunately, the meeting takes place before her party. I think her suspicions would be bristling if she knew we were in the city."

"She thinks yer dead," Tobin pointed out.

"True. Perhaps I will not shave until after the party." He sat back and thought for a moment. "I can use that to my advantage. I can sneak in, and if caught, I have plenty of excuses. I have been playing the peddling delivery boy for some time now, and some of her servants will recognize me."

Tobin shook his head. "I think it is too dangerous. Wellington will not like it."

"He trusts me," Philip retorted.

"To not be an ejeet." Tobin held up his hands. "But you are my superior. What do ye want me to do?"

"Play a vagrant in the alleyway. Watch who is coming and going."

"Easy enough," Tobin agreed. "I should probably start now. Where do I find disguises around here?"

"I happen to know a place and a seamstress," Philip said with a grin.

"ARE WE ARRIVING UNANNOUNCED?" Meg asked the Duke once they were on their way to Dover.

"I debated whether it might be advisable to arrive in Paris and hope we would cross paths, but I believe it would be more advantageous to make it appear it is a friendly, family visit. I sent a note, announcing our sojourn in Paris and making it known that her nieces desire to become acquainted."

"That is clever and true, for Amelia at least," Meg replied.

"You do not desire to know her better?" Amelia asked.

"Perhaps, one day I may do, but my feelings are still very bruised from our previous encounter. She did release Tobin, and for that I am grateful, but the life she chose to live I cannot approve of."

"I think we should give her a chance. You yourself did things you would not have imagined, in order to protect me."

"I admit I would never have thought to be a kitchen maid, but it hardly compares to being the most famous courtesan in France, nor to using people to spy on their governments."

"She did not murder our parents, however; our uncle did," Amelia retorted.

"That is true. What she did was patriotic. It is no different from our soldiers trying to ascertain Napoleon's intentions," the Duke added.

"In the same way you and Captain Elliot did, during the war?" Amelia asked.

Waverley inclined his head. "Along with many others."

"Are you trying to dismiss my aunt's behaviour?" Meg asked, taken aback. "All I have heard is how dangerous she is, and now you want me to act as though nothing has happened?"

"Not at all, my love. I think you should be yourself. However, I understand Amelia's fascination, and I want you to keep an open mind—listen to her side of the tale if she tries to explain more. You never know when she might divulge something useful to England."

Meg looked out of the window and crossed her arms. "I suppose she did what she thought she had to do. Our mother was more fortunate in her choice of brothers, so I will try to be conciliating."

The carriage pulled to a stop. They had reached Dover, where a hired yacht was waiting to take them to France. Amelia's heart skipped a beat. She knew Meg was reluctant to go, but she could not be more excited. This was even better than going to London had been.

Three days later, they reached Paris, and not a moment too soon. The Duke had insisted on travelling slowly due to Meg's condition, and they had had to wait until she felt better each morning in order to travel. If that was what being with child entailed, Amelia was happy to wait!

As they entered through the *Porte d'Auteuil*, the anticipation grew. It was not unlike London at first—open countryside with farms, becoming more crowded, with houses close together, as they drew near to the city. The beauty of the architecture stole the breath, and a river flowed through the centre, much like London. Yet the Seine seemed cleaner and more romantic, with bright flower boxes of yellow and purple pansies hanging from window-sills. They travelled alongside the water and over stone bridges before they reached the streets with the famous shops. Amelia simply stared out of the window in fascination. "Look at the milliners! And the modistes!"

Waverley groaned.

"Did you think you could bring us to Paris and expect us not to go shopping?"

He did not bother to comment. "That is *Le Arc de Triomphe de l'Étoile*," he pointed out instead.

"It is beautiful!" Meg said, appearing to be equally entranced.

"We are close, now. Your aunt's house is not far from the palace and Wellington's residence."

"How very convenient," Meg murmured.

"But of course."

"May we drive by the palace?" Amelia asked.

"We will do so in a few moments. There it is, on your right." It was hard to take in all of the palace when driving by in a carriage.

"And your aunt's house is over there," he pointed to a modern *hôtel* on the Rue Cambon, which was a white stone, Palladian building and looked similar to many in London.

"Why do they allow vagrants here?" Amelia asked, frowning at a dirty beggar loitering outside her aunt's home.

"They are everywhere," he answered, gazing at the object of her consternation. "He is more likely to receive a few coins from a rich man passing then a poor man in the slums."

"I expect so, but it ruins my perfect view," she retorted with impudence.

"They all do, my dear, but I imagine they would trade places with you," he said, a large smile on his face.

"Very droll," she replied, not thinking it humorous at all.

"And here we are," he said a few moments later as they slowed before a house that looked worthy to be a ducal palace.

Within minutes, there was a flurry of footmen, postilions and servants, rushing to take the horses and carry the luggage into the house.

Amelia stopped and looked upward, turning in a circle to admire the beauty and absorb every detail.

"It smells different here," she said to no one in particular, and yet unable to describe the difference. As she stood, lost in her surroundings, someone ran into her and she almost lost her balance. "Another vagrant!" she exclaimed. "Watch where you are going, sirrah!"

The person had the audacity to turn and tip his hat to her. She even thought she detected white teeth smiling at her from the beneath the bushy beard he wore. He certainly left a stench behind.

She gasped at his audacity before a notion struck her. There was something familiar about him. Staring after him well past the time she could no longer see him, she had to wonder...

"No. It could not be." She shook her head.

"What could not be, my dear?" Amelia turned to see the Duke of Wellington himself standing in front of her, looking vastly amused.

"I thought I saw... oh, never mind. I must be fatigued from the journey, sir. My mind is playing tricks on me."

"You never know," he said, his eyes twinkling, as he held out his arm to her and began to walk in towards the steps leading up to the front entrance. "Forgive me the impertinence of introducing myself.

Waverley has already taken your sister inside and given me the honour of escorting you."

She looked up at him and gave him her most brilliant smile. "Everyone knows who you are, your Grace." And it was true. He was the most famous person in England, probably liked even more than the king.

"You have made quite a name for yourself, as well," he chuckled. "I can see I will need to keep you away from my soldiers or they will never listen to me."

"Oh, please do not do that, sir! I was so looking forward to your famous balls!"

"Well, in that case, maybe I will allow you to meet a few of them. We are not facing any great battles at the moment, so some distraction might be good for them. You must promise to save the first dance tonight for me."

"Tonight?

A butler opened the door for them and he escorted her inside.

"Yes, your aunt is holding a soirée. Welcome to my Paris home, Lady Amelia."

CHAPTER 4

*P*hilip really should not have teased Lady Amelia, but at the time he could not seem to help himself. She was so young and full of joy, and something about her made him forget about the seriousness of his task. Even if she recognized him now, he would be himself again that evening.

He laughed as he walked along the Rue Saint Honoré. She had been so annoyed when he bumped into her! It would be entertaining to have her present during this assignment, but he was wary of having her underfoot and in danger. It would require all of his attention to make sure she was safe and not distracting him from his true purpose.

The avenue was busy with pedestrians and deliveries. A candle maker and the milk maids made deliveries, and other sundries were also brought to the larger houses. Philip spied Tobin in a corner across the street from La Glacier's house and had to admit the Irishman was playing his part well. There were other beggars and a group of pie sellers in the vicinity, so he was inconspicuous. Philip crossed the street to where Tobin was at his post. He bought two meat pies from the nearby vendor and checked his surroundings. After he was certain Tobin had seen him, he walked past him into the alleyway. A few minutes passed before Tobin joined him.

"Are you going to share?"

"Are you hungry?" Philip taunted as he held a pie up to his mouth.

"Of course I am hungry, you worthless *gobshite*. I could hardly buy a pie when I am supposed to have no money. I have been tortured by the smell for hours now."

"I suppose I could share," Philip said, handing him one of the pies.

Tobin grabbed the food from Philip and devoured it. Philip handed him the second one and Tobin looked up in surprise.

"I had a good breakfast."

Tobin scowled at Philip, but took the pie and ate it. When he had finished, Philip finally got down to business.

"Do you have anything for me?"

"No. So far it has been quiet. It makes me wonder if they are to have the meeting here, after all. Should there not be extra traffic?"

Philip frowned. "It is about time, and she is having a party here tonight. There should at least be extra deliveries as well as signs of cleaning and other preparations. Who is watching the back?"

"I do not ken. My post is in the front."

"I will see what I can discover. She has probably moved the location."

"Where else would it be? They could hardly hold it at the palace."

"I have no idea, but I intend to find out. Send word if anything changes," Philip directed.

"Yes, sir," Tobin said with a hint of mockery in his voice. Philip ignored him and went on to explore at the rear of the house. However, there was no sign of any activity in the alleyway behind the *hôtel*. A large stone wall stood guard around the courtyard, but for a house holding a party that evening, something did not hold true. It should be a hive of activity.

"She is trying to fool us," he murmured to himself, "but will the meeting really be here and she is trying to make us think it will be somewhere else, or is it actually to be somewhere else?"

Philip knocked on the service door for deliveries. After several minutes, a young maid finally answered.

"*Oui?*"

Philip attempted his charming, flirtatious persona. "I heard there was a party tonight. I have come to offer my services," he said with a wink.

"And what services would those be, *Monsieur?*" she asked, rightfully sceptical.

"I am a man of many talents. I will do anything."

"I will have to ask the housekeeper. We do have a party here tonight, but my mistress is very particular about who she allows to work for her."

"Very understandable. Is there anything I can do to help before the party?" He rolled up his sleeves and flexed his hands. "I am not afraid of any job," he said, raising his eyebrows and flashing her a smile. "It is hard to find work with the Emperor in exile. I was one of his devoted soldiers," Philip added in a pitiful tone.

"I am certain my mistress would be pleased to hire you, but she is gone out for the day."

"And your housekeeper?"

The maid looked around to see if anyone was listening. "She pretends to be in charge, but she does nothing without the mistress's approval."

"Oh, I see. What is so important for the mistress to be out all day when she has a grand party at her house tonight?"

"Who can say? She is a very important person."

"You are fortunate to work for her, then. I hope the rumours are true about the army rising up again. I had heard Madame was organizing the cause. Perhaps another day I may speak with her."

"You may wait for her, if you wish, but it is not likely she will have time to meet with you today. Her man, Lannes, is more likely to have time, but unfortunately, he also went out."

"Maybe one day I can be a part of their important plans."

"I wish I could help you more. Perhaps you could try tomorrow?"

"Yes, tomorrow."

"Should I tell her you called?"

"It would do no good. I have no card or direction. I will try again tomorrow as you say. *Au revoir.*"

The gate closed behind him and Philip muttered a curse to himself. He was so close! Was the maid an excellent liar? Was she privy to her mistresses whereabouts?

Either way, it seemed she was not going to divulge anything else. Pondering his next course of action, he was walking slowly back along the alleyway when an open door caught his attention. It was in the ground, but it did not look as if it led to a sewer. The steps were made of stone and led back in the direction of where La Glacier's house loomed above the kennel. He glanced around him from beneath his hat. Seeing no one, he looked down a few steps and heard voices, but none he recognized. If this was the meeting, where were the look-outs? He went back up to the street. It would do no good to be caught now. There had to be guards somewhere—obviously they were relaxing in their duties. Was there a tunnel close, perchance, whereby he could try to get closer and listen to what was going forward?

At the end of the road, he finally found one. He lifted the cover and made his way down into the sewers. It was easy to become disoriented and the stench was as bad as anything he had ever experienced. Wading through murky waste and liquid, he tried to count out which house must be La Glacier's. By his best estimate, he was somewhere between her house and the tunnels leading toward the palace. He found what appeared to be a room of stone, but no entrance from the east sewage tunnels.

Skirting around the edge for any way to listen in, he had almost made it around the perimeter of this cellar when he found a small vent.

"That is all for now, then," La Glacier said, sounding hollow. "We continue to amass the army and wait for the emperor's return."

"Vivre l'Empereur'!" the men shouted.

"Now, I must prepare for my unexpected visitors. I will send word when it is time for our next move. We must continue to be patient and vigilant."

Philip waited as the people began to disperse. He could make out very little through the small vent, only chairs being pushed back from a table. He needed to get back to Wellington and report, quickly. He waded through the muck back to the street, going one street further, closer to where Tobin was camped, and climbed the small ladder up to fresh air.

"What happened to ye?" Tobin asked, making a face and covering his nose.

"I have been in the sewers, eavesdropping."

"Whatever takes yer fancy. Madame returned to the house five minutes ago. It looked as though she had been shopping."

"She is very clever, since she was doing nothing of the sort. I am back to Headquarters if you want to go."

"What, and leave my post of luxury and intrigue?" he mocked.

"Suit yourself. I am off to take a bath and shave."

"I will be along soon. It would not do to be seen together."

"Very well. I will give my report on the meeting to the Duke by myself."

"Ye were listening to the meeting?" Tobin asked in a hushed voice. "Why did ye not say so?"

Philip grinned and walked south, away from the Rue Cambon towards the Rue Saint Honoré.

When he arrived he chose the servants' entrance, to the dismay of all in his path. He left his boots, stockings and outer clothing outside the door.

"Burn those clothes, send up a bath to my rooms as soon as possible and tell the Duke I need to speak with him urgently—as soon as I have washed."

"*Oui, Monsieur.*"

Philip was soaking the stench away in a copper bath next to the fire when, without ceremony, Wellington burst into his room. His magnificent presence seemed to fill what space was left of the chamber.

Philip made to stand, but Wellington waved him back down. "What did you discover?"

"I only happened upon the meeting by surprise. It was in a secret chamber, down among the tunnels between the palace and La Glacier's residence. I could not gain entrance to the house, and I only discovered it as I was leaving. The door to the alley was left open."

"A lucky chance, by God, but I will take it. What did they say?"

"I only arrived for the end, but it seems they are amassing an army for Napoleon's expected return. There was no mention of a date, but the group shouted, "'Vivre l'Empereur' before they left."

"Ha. Wishful thinking. I do not mind if they waste their time indulging in fancy, but consider this: will they appoint a new leader instead? We must be prepared, Elliot," Wellington barked. "I will send my man to you. No need to look like a bear any longer."

DESPITE HAVING the latest fashions in London, Amelia was dissatisfied with her current wardrobe when she would be attending a ball with the elite in Paris.

Amelia and Meg were in the Duchess' dressing room, a surprisingly feminine space done in gold and green. They were trying to decide what would be suitable, when Waverley knocked on the door.

"May I come in?" he asked, somewhat unnecessarily since he was already stepping over the threshold.

"Of course," Meg said.

"I have received a letter from your aunt."

"What does it say?"

"It is a personal invitation to her gathering tonight. Instead of being guests of Wellington, we will be there at her behest."

"That is for the best. I am glad she sent a note. Amelia is concerned, however, that we do not have the latest Parisian fashions," Meg explained to her husband.

"You have the latest London fashions. They will be just as curious to see how you look as you are wishful to be approved. It is all in how you present yourself."

Meg agreed but Amelia was not convinced, and looked at him sceptically.

"No one will be looking at your gown," the Duke reassured her.

"Lavender, cerulean, or pomona?" she asked, holding up three gowns beneath her chin.

"Lavender is my favourite colour," Meg answered.

"Then lavender it shall be," she said sweetly. "Will there be French officers present?"

"I assume you are asking for information's sake, not romantic notions," Waverley remarked with a frown.

"Of course not! I want to be alert and help discover whatever it is that needs to be discovered. It would be useful to know what information we seek, precisely."

Waverley sighed deeply and sat down in one of the armchairs. "That is often the great difficulty with being a spy. You do not always know what you are looking for. Wellington has suspicions, but since Napoleon is on the island of Elba, under guard, we cannot definitively say he is organizing another army against the rest of Europe."

"Yet you have your suspicions?"

"Rumour has it that King Louis has not regained the support or trust of the people, and that they are still loyal to Napoleon."

"So we are merely here to set a foot inside the door and report anything we hear?"

"Yes, Wellington is not above using every tool available to him to win, which I respect, except in cases when it involves my family. I want you both to promise me that you will do nothing stupid. Do not go anywhere alone."

"I would have no notion where to go," Amelia protested, holding out her hands.

"Trust me, it will happen—more than once, no doubt. You are naturally curious, which can make for an excellent spy, but if you do not know your own limitations, you will die. Any of these people will be willing to kill in the name of their country."

Amelia's heart sped up at the realization they might be involved in intrigue and danger.

"How will I get information to you if I hear anything? It is you I come to, I collect?"

Waverley wrinkled his face. "I assume so, but Wellington might give you some other people you can go to if I am not available. You need a signal to make if you are in distress."

"What kind of signal?" she asked.

"Some kind of subtle gesture, like pulling on your necklace or juggling your earring."

"I see. I tend to play with my necklace when I am nervous, so it had better not to be that. My earrings then. If I play with my earrings, then that shall be my sign." She demonstrated the movement.

"Do I need one, too?" Meg asked.

"I do not intend to let you out of my sight, but I suppose it is a wise precaution."

"Then mine will be my necklace. I do not normally play with it."

"Is there anyone in particular you expect to be here who we should become acquainted with?" Amelia asked.

"Only your aunt. I have been told of no one else of any particular interest. We assume her closest advisers will be there. Napoleon's main man, Lannes, is now by her side for the most part. Her circle is very small."

"How will I know who everyone is?"

"You will be introduced to everyone you need to know," he assured her.

Amelia took a deep breath and wiped her clammy hands on her skirts.

"The key to being a spy is for no one to have any idea what you are doing. Pretend you are going to your first London ball and plan on capturing everyone's interest. You have the natural gift of drawing attention to yourself, so pretend you are a happy *ingénue* with naught on her mind except catching the biggest prize."

"I wish that was what was on her mind," Meg remarked dryly.

"Unfair, sister!" Amelia wailed.

"I will leave you two to dress. I am certain it is a good time for me to withdraw." Waverley held up his hand defensively and left the room. As soon as the Duke was out of the door, Meg set her arms around Amelia.

"I do not want you to do this!" she cried.

"I will be all right. I will be careful, I promise."

She shook her head. "You do not know how these people behave. They are ruthless! I saw with my own eyes what they did to people who they believed had crossed them."

"I gathered some notion when they kidnapped me."

"Forgive me. Of course you did."

"My country needs me, and I will do the best I can. I may not be able to help at all, but I will get to know our aunt and that is enough, if nothing else. I miss our parents, Meg."

"I do too, Amelia, but recollect it is our aunt who is responsible for their deaths!"

"No, it was our sick, traitorous uncle! His twisted infatuation with her did that. He wanted money and power to impress her. Do you believe she would have ordered the death of her own sister?"

"I could not say," Meg answered quietly. "I would not like to believe it of her. I could never do such a thing."

Amelia reached over and stroked her sister's hand. "Nor I, but this is simple enough for us to do. So I will do it."

"Please be careful. I cannot bear to lose you, too."

Some minutes later, they dried the tears which had then overtaken them both and Meg left her to dress for the evening. Amelia wore a gown in a shade of dark lavender, with a soft, flowing organza fabric that moved with her when she walked. The neck descended to a 'v' at the front of the bodice, with a slight sleeve over the shoulder of the same flowing fabric. Simple pearls with matching ear-drops—she would never look at earrings in the same way again—and her hair pulled back in a severe knot, with a pearl circlet around her head, completed her toilet. After donning her slippers and choosing her reticule, she looked at herself in the glass.

She felt older, more mature. It was time for a new chapter in her life. She would leave her fantasies of Captain Elliot behind with the child she had been when newly from the schoolroom. It was time to grow up and take on the serious task before her.

How would she feel if she was the cause of her aunt's demise?

"Wretched," she answered herself. Was this the kind of coldness spies had to assume to do their duty? It was probably much worse than she could imagine, she acknowledged to herself, yet she felt up to the task. She wanted and needed to do something worthwhile with her life. If it meant sacrificing it for the good of her country, so be it. After a Season in London, though, she did not know if she could force herself to make a loveless match for the sake of alliance. A sinking feeling came over her, and she knew it was nervousness. When she walked through the door, she would be accepting a new way of life.

"Amelia, my girl, into the breach!" she encouraged herself. Her looks and form were pleasing, she knew that. "Thank God for lavender, His gift to all redheads."

With nothing else to do to delay any longer, she went out of the door, across the grand hallway, and down the red-carpeted stairs to meet her party.

"Lady Amelia, at last," Wellington said brusquely, looking at her with blatant appreciation.

"If one of his soldiers was thus late, he would be given slop duty, Captain Frome said, coming forward to greet her, looking dashing in his Regimentals.

"I did not know you were joining us!" Amelia said, holding out her hand to him.

"London was not the same without you, my dear."

She gave him a look of doubt. "I am certain it has lost no time in speculating on my leaving, however."

He conceded her point with an incline of his head.

"Shall we go?" Wellington encouraged as the butler opened the door.

"I think we are forgetting someone," Waverley remarked. Amelia turned to see another gentleman she had not noticed before, standing behind them.

"Lady Amelia, we meet again," he said jovially, stepping forward to bow to her.

"Captain Elliot?"

CHAPTER 5

This assignment would see him dead, he was convinced, from the moment he saw Lady Amelia walk down the stairs. She was even more striking with her dark red locks than her renowned aunt, and every eye in Paris would be upon her wherever she went. It was like that with beauty, especially when combined with a disposition that was not quite like that of her sister, but that made your heart sing loud tunes.

Despite his years of training to be unaffected, he could feel his reaction to her. His blood was rushing through his veins, and some kind of feeling akin to drunken happiness swept over him. She would assuredly be the death of him if he could not control himself—and Wellington wanted him to be her nursemaid? This would never do. True enough, he had worked with other beautiful women while on assignments, but she was different. He did not know why, but he did not like it. Philip knew he was not marriageable material, yet he could not carry on a simple flirtation either. There was nothing but hell and damnation in his future—and Lady Amelia was too closely related to Waverley.

Amelia did not even notice him when she came down the stairs.

Trust Frome to steal her attention, he thought unfairly, but he knew James was as big a flirt as he was himself.

By Jove, she was more breathtaking the closer she came! She only looked amused by James's machinations, and did not appear to be taking him seriously. Was she already so jaded by one Season? By all accounts, she had received several marriage proposals from the biggest catches on the market. Waverley had even said she had run away from Wadsworth's attempt to force her hand. Philip was becoming more intrigued by the moment—another bad omen for him. Once he was put on a trail, he had an impossible time abandoning it.

Waverley pointed him out, curse him. Philip was enjoying his observations. Nevertheless, he stepped forward.

"Lady Amelia, we meet again."

"Captain Elliot?" She looked at him as though she had seen a ghost. Had they not told her he was alive? Not that he had spent much time with her to leave much of an impression. His recollection was of her beauty, but also her youth and innocence. She had lost some of that innocence, upon closer inspection, no longer looking at the world in awe. Instead of continuing to stand foolishly, staring awkwardly, he held out his arm.

"Shall we go? My Commander loves punctuality as much as he loves beautiful women."

That drew a laugh from her. Good. He would have to keep her laughing and smiling.

They settled into one of Wellington's town chariots across from the Duke and Duchess. Since the couple were absorbed in each other, he spoke to Lady Amelia.

"Have you forgotten me?"

She turned and looked at him, eyes wide with disbelief. "Forgotten you, Captain? How could we? We thought you might be dead, and people were searching for you everywhere."

"I had the good fortune to see you only once before I left for France. It would not be surprising if you had."

She looked away, out of the window. They had almost arrived, but he waited for her response. He must have said the wrong thing.

Instead of ringing a peal over his head, she merely whispered, "I did not forget you," before the carriage halted. The door opened, curtailing further conversation as a footman handed both ladies down.

Philip watched as La Glacier made a grand spectacle of leaving her post at the top of the stairs and coming down the steps, past those already waiting to greet her nieces. As much indeed, he reflected, as the 'ice queen' ever made spectacles. Elegant and composed as ever, she appeared to great advantage this evening being dressed in all white with pearls in her light hair, enhancing the striking pale blue of her eyes.

"*Mes nièces!*" she exclaimed as she held out her arms.

Philip escorted Lady Amelia to La Glacier's side and made to go. Curiously, Amelia held onto him for a moment before releasing him. Waverley also had the Duchess by his side and seemed reluctant to let go of her until she gave him a subtle nod.

Both men stepped back and watched.

Standing next to each other, the resemblance between the three ladies was uncanny. The Duchess's colouring was identical to her aunt's, but it was Amelia whom embodied La Glacier's nature.

"It would be difficult to find three more beautiful specimens in one place," Philip remarked

"You allowed me to think you were dead all this time and that is the first thing you can say to me?" Waverley threw him a look of disbelief and received an air of insouciance in return.

"You know how the service is. I did send word once I thought it was safe to do so," Philip replied in quick defence.

He could see that Waverley was containing his emotion. Briefly closing his eyes, the Duke swallowed hard.

"I had a feeling, deep inside, that you might still be alive. It is why I sent Tobin to search for you."

Knowing it was hurtful causing Waverley to speak thus, Philip fought for composure.

"Tobin did an excellent job. He was within feet of me on numerous occasions."

Waverley closed his eyes again and exhaled. "You could have trusted him."

"It was not a matter of trust."

Waverley gave him a sideways look.

Philip shrugged one shoulder in the French manner he had adopted. "Perhaps there was a certain amount of distrust."

"The two of you will be working together a great deal, so I suggest you put aside whatever reservations you have about him."

"I will admit that I cannot fault his efforts thus far. By the by, where is the Irish rascal now?"

"He wanted to continue his post as a vagrant. He thought he could be more useful that way."

To himself at least, Philip had to admit he was surprised. Perhaps the fellow would do after all.

"As far as Amelia goes," the Duke was saying, "please be careful."

"I am always careful," Philip said through his teeth. They had not been alone since they had arrived and had not had the opportunity to broach the personal topics of the assignment.

"I am not impugning your honour," Waverley said mildly.

"Pray tell, then, what is your meaning?"

"How do I say this without affecting everything?" He looked around.

Philip glared at the back of Waverley's head and waited for the answer.

"I will say, simply, that you made an impression on Amelia when you met in London. She never quite forgot you."

Philip stared. He was not quite certain what that meant.

"Need I spell it out for you?" Waverley prompted.

"I suppose you do. It does not seem possible that a female who, by all accounts, has every man in London at her feet would have harboured a tendre for me on such short acquaintance."

"Perhaps not, but you went missing not long after her kidnapping, and I imagine it was romanticized in her mind."

"No. I cannot believe it of her," he said, looking over to the object of their discussion. "She does not behave as though she is moonstruck over me."

"Believe what you wish, but I wanted you to be aware of the situation since Wellington has decided to appoint you her protector on this commission. I do not intend to be far away, but in this capacity it will be difficult for me to be with her at all times."

"I need a drink," Philip said absent-mindedly as he tried to reconcile these revelations.

"No, you must remain alert. You know that."

"I do not like any of this one bit. I do not see why Wellington thought to bring the sisters in. It is too dangerous and I was close to getting inside."

"We will never be able to get as close as her own flesh and blood can. She is, in truth, like ice... except with them. I would not have thought it possible had I not seen it on the ship last year. She was a different person entirely when she spoke to Meg."

Philip knew what his friend said was true; he had seen it with his own eyes.

"Here they come," Waverley said as La Glacier walked towards them with Meg and Amelia on either side of her.

"Captain Elliot, you come as a guest this time?" La Glacier asked, eyeing him with evident amusement.

"How could I stay away with such beauty near?"

She glanced at Amelia and then back to him. "*Oui*, I cannot blame you. Be careful, *Monsieur*."

AMELIA WATCHED her aunt glide away to her other guests, leaving her standing beside Captain Elliot. So many emotions were swirling inside her, she wanted to go somewhere secluded and be alone before she made a fool of herself. She did not want to face him.

"Penny for your thoughts?" Captain Elliot asked, a thread of humour running through his quiet tone.

"I am not even certain what they are," she said frankly, avoiding his gaze. She could not speak honestly about her feelings, at any rate, because she knew how ridiculous she had been in pining for him all these months.

"It must be fascinating, meeting your infamous aunt after everything that has happened."

Amelia watched that aunt, holding court across the room, as every other person, male and female, watched the magnetic figure. She was fascinating. Her beauty was much like Meg's but more refined and elusive. She wore a slim-fitting gown of white that sparkled like diamonds as she moved, seeming to float everywhere she went. It was easy to see why Napoleon wanted her.

"I suppose so," she answered. "She is very like my mother, yet very unlike her."

"They have led two very different lives."

"My aunt had little choice." Amelia found herself defending a person she scarcely knew.

Captain Elliot looked at her curiously. "A person always has a choice."

She was finding herself growing angry with him and she knew it was not fair, but she felt it anyway. He had scarcely noticed her before he left for France, just as Meg had warned, yet she had felt an attachment to him which had affected her deeply. Now, here they were, and she wanted to be far away from him, but he was so close she could feel his warmth and smell his cologne of citrus and musk.

"Lady Amelia?" he prompted.

"I beg your pardon," she said, realizing she was being inattentive and unforgivably rude.

"Are you feeling unwell? Would you like me to escort you back?"

"No, no, thank you. I am not ill, only a little shocked."

"Which is perfectly understandable," he said gently.

"It is hard to believe my aunt is all they say she is." They watched La Glacier, looking like any hostess at a Society ball in London. Except for her being dressed in unrelieved white, it felt perfectly normal.

"That is a subject you and I need to speak on, but this is not the place." He leaned forward and spoke quietly.

"I do not know when you would like to speak, but my time here is short. My aunt has just invited me to leave with her in the morning, to go to her country estate."

"Alone?" he asked.

"Waverley and my sister are also coming."

"Then we must talk now. It is urgent."

Amelia did not want to talk and especially not with him, over whom her emotions were still in flux. The heart was such a fickle creature; only a few hours before she had been dreaming of finding him!

"Very well. Shall we seek another, quieter place, or shall we dance?"

"Mayhap we should dance?" he remarked. "We are less likely to be overheard that way."

Amelia saw him subtly scan the room full of people and glanced up at him suspiciously. Nonetheless, she took his proffered arm.

"Pretend you like me," Captain Elliot commanded while guiding her through the guests to the dance floor.

"I do not dislike you," she explained. "I simply was not expecting to see you."

"Why should you expect to see me? Although I hope my sister will be better pleased, I do not believe she is expecting to see me either."

"Poor Adelaide." Amelia clicked her tongue and shook her head.

"You are acquainted with my sister?" Captain Elliot looked taken aback.

"The best of friends." She nodded her head. "We braved London together, though she was fortunate to find a man to love and comfort her."

Captain Elliot pulled her close and began waltzing with her, despite the fact that no one else was dancing yet, and the music was more in the background than for a formal dance. She could no longer avoid looking into his midnight blue eyes framed by his black hair hanging across his brow. It was just like in her dreams.

"You are holding me too close, sir," she reprimanded.

"*Au contraire*. We are in Paris and we need to pretend we are young and in love." The skin around his eyes crinkled, charm oozing from every limb.

Amelia's heart almost stopped. "Why must we do such a thing?" she asked, though she complied and stopped resisting his close hold on her.

"Because I need to be invited to your aunt's country estate, and the only way to obtain such an invitation is as your favoured beau."

Amelia was certain her cheeks were flaming. She was already embarrassed and out of sorts, being so close to Captain Elliot; indeed, she could hardly think coherently. And now he was proposing they pretend to be in love?

He was watching her closely which was all the more disconcerting.

"Are you spying on my aunt?" She had leaned forward to whisper in his ear and thought he shivered beneath her hands, before deciding she must be mistaken.

"I am a soldier, Lady Amelia. I assume you have been told why Wellington has asked you here?"

She gave a slight nod.

"His Grace believes you and I can work together more efficiently."

"I collect, he thinks I need a guardian," she snapped.

"Those are your words, my lady, not mine." He spun her about but she refused to be distracted.

"Do you disagree?"

"I think you have never done such a thing before. Even seasoned spies need guidance and a partner to look out for them.

"You would be my partner?" She tried to hold the disbelief from her voice.

"Now is the time to object before anyone leaves Paris. If you are not equal to the task, we must know now."

She needed to be alone to think. Her thoughts were so very conflicted while in his arms.

"You were not aware spying was really acting upon a dangerous stage, did you?"

Amelia laughed. It was too much to believe. "I cannot believe what I am hearing."

"I confess I was also surprised to learn of Wellington's plan."

"I cannot imagine it pleased you to hear you were to be partnered with me."

"I will not be made to confess anything of the sort, my lady." He pulled back and kissed her hand in a lingering manner before taking her arm and leading her back to her sister. "Consider the matter carefully and let me know your decision as soon as you may tomorrow morning."

She would hardly do anything else!

La Glacier—Aunt Lisette—then walked over to greet her as Captain Elliot strode away.

"I was unaware you and the Captain had formed an attachment."

It seemed she would not have a chance to think after all, Amelia mused. "We became acquainted before my uncle kidnapped me, ma'am. We were unable to further that acquaintance due to unfortunate events. Now, it seems, fate has brought us together again." She allowed her eyes to follow him in what she hoped was a longing fashion.

Meg was trying to remain impassive but Amelia could read the disapproval in her eyes. Waverley merely looked amused. His mouth lifted slightly and the skin around his eyes crinkled.

"Perhaps we could stay in Paris for a while longer?" Amelia suggested, knowing it was a risk.

"I daresay another day or two would not hurt, but my estate is much nicer this time of year."

"Merci, Aunt. I would like a chance..." She let her voice trail off.

"I understand. I was young once."

"You are still young," Amelia protested.

"*La*, it is much too late for me, *ma belle*. My purpose in life, now, is far greater than myself. Enjoy your beau, but do not limit yourself yet awhile. Some men are not meant to be domesticated—which is why they are so irresistible."

"My eyes are open, Aunt. I simply wish to enjoy my visit to Paris."

"As long as you are wise, I do not see the harm. In fact, if, in two days' time, you still wish it, you may bring him to my estate. I will not be the cause of your wishing he were there."

"You are the best of aunts!" Amelia exclaimed and kissed her on the cheek.

La Glacier smiled a genuine smile. Amelia could see her mother in her aunt. It made her soften towards the woman and want to know her better.

Aunt Lisette was then distracted by her man, Lannes, who whispered in her ear and pulled her away.

"That was cleverly done, Amelia," Waverley said.

"I do not like it," Meg objected. "I can see you are already softening towards her."

"She does remind me of Mother when she smiles. There is good in her, I am sure."

"I have not said there was not, but I have seen what she is capable of," Meg argued.

"And I have heard," Amelia retorted. "I will be careful."

"What of Captain Elliot?" Meg prodded. "Can you work so closely with him?"

"We understand each other."

"I hope so, Amelia. I hope so."

CHAPTER 6

$\mathcal{T}$he next morning, Philip rose early. He had not spoken to Lady Amelia again the night before, but Waverley had sent him a note telling him they were spending two days in Paris and then he would be invited to the fortress. He had to give Lady Amelia credit for that much, at least.

What he could not reconcile, however, was what Waverley had said about her having a tendre for him and her behaviour last night. She had seemed as though she would rather he go to the devil than court her.

He poured a cup of coffee and found himself looking into it, trying to decide what approach to take with her.

"Your coffee will grow cold if you keep staring at it," a familiar voice warned. Turning at once, Philip sped to the doorway, and gathering his sister in his arms, spun her around.

She laughed. "Put me down before I lose my stomach!"

Philip set her down and then held her at arm's length. "Let me look at you, Mrs. Fielding." She had his same ebony hair and bright blue eyes. They looked like twins.

"So, you have heard, then?"

"I would have been there, Addy. I did not know."

"I did not know you were alive at the time, either," she reprimanded.

He took her hand, led her to a chair and handed her into it.

"We have much to catch up on. Would you care for some coffee?"

"No, I think some tea would do better," she replied, patting her stomach.

"So soon?"

"We have been married a few months already, you know." She smiled, clearly thinking of her new husband.

"I am glad to see you happy, and I will be equally glad to be an uncle."

He rang for some tea, and then sat down beside her in some chairs placed on the veranda overlooking the gardens.

"I tried to send word, Addy. For a while, it was safer to have people think me dead."

"And now?"

"Wellington has a different plan for me."

"When will you come home, Philip?"

"I cannot say. There is still enough of a threat that I am needed here."

Adelaide looked away, but not before Philip saw tears pooling in her eyes. He reached over and squeezed her hand.

"Forgive me. I am more emotional these days, but it does not change the fact that you are the only family I have left. When I thought I had lost you..."

"You have Fielding. I am grateful you found such an honourable man; and you have created a new life to shower your love upon."

"What you say is true, but do not belittle the bond we share," she argued.

"Never would I. However, I will not ever be able to lead a life of domestic bliss such as you and Fielding have. I am not a rich man of great property. I am but a soldier."

"Robert and I wanted to speak with you about that. I was supposed to wait for him. He thinks I will make a mull of it."

"No. I will not accept charity, much though I appreciate the offer."

"Will you not even hear what it is?" She was clearly hurt. "It is not charity!"

He looked away, clenching his jaw. His father had always provided for them, and he had never desired what so many of his peers had because of the happiness and love in their home, which most of his friends did not have. His home was where his schoolmates wished to visit during holidays. Yet there were times when he was reminded of what he could not have now, and so he engrossed himself in serving his country.

"At the very least, know that the money you had intended for me upon your death is still in the bank. It is untouched and will remain so by my husband and myself. It has grown into rather a substantial sum, I believe."

"I had forgotten about that. I expect that means the estate sold well, if there is a goodly competence?"

"No, it means the funds were invested wisely. The estate is still there for you. Robert has been overseeing its care, and there are tenants residing there until you should wish to return to it."

Philip ought to be angry that his wishes had not been honoured, but instead he felt some measure of relief he had something to go back to, even if it was not a grand property. It was still his home.

"Thank you, Addy. That was all intended for you. I did not expect to return."

"I know why you made those arrangements, but I refused to accept such a bequest then and I still do. I want my children to visit their uncle and see where I grew up."

He felt his throat grow tight and was forced to change the subject before he became a sobbing fool.

"How long do you intend to stay in Paris?"

She smiled at him as though she knew what he was doing. "Only a few days. Robert has business to tend to in England, but he would not deny me seeing you in the flesh."

"Good man. Where is he?" He looked around.

"In the library, giving us time alone."

"Then let me go and greet my new brother." He helped his sister up from her chair, and they walked down the hall to the library.

When they entered the room, several others were already there. Tobin was speaking, reporting that a large entourage had left La Glacier's house early that morning.

"I did not expect a crowd at such an hour," Philip remarked once the assembled stopped their discussions and turned their attention upon him.

Captain Frome, Tobin, Waverley and Fielding were there. They all stood up at Adelaide's presence. Fielding came forward to take his wife's arm and shake his new brother's hand.

"Welcome to the family," Philip greeted. "Adelaide seems happy and therefore I am happy, not that she would have accepted my objections, mind you."

"You are alive and that is all that matters, now," Fielding replied.

"You are not about to harangue me for allowing her to believe I was dead?" Philip asked, surprised.

"I am certain she has already done that." He chuckled.

Adelaide sat down and the men followed. "I briefly mentioned our plan, husband, but did not have the opportunity to finish explaining," she said, casting a quelling look at her brother.

"Then you arrive with perfect timing," Fielding said. "I was beginning to explain it to these gentlemen."

"Pray tell. What is this madness?" Philip asked as he took a seat near the door.

"As all of you are aware, I dabble in trade, mainly imports and exports."

The gentlemen inclined their heads.

"Do you perhaps recall Captain Abbott?" Various murmurings of assent greeted the question. "His father, Sir Charles has tobacco plantations in Virginia. He intends to return to England soon and turn his plantations over to his daughter, Elinor. He wishes to establish trustworthy trading partners, and Captain Abbott suggested me."

"I know the Abbotts. Capital family," Waverley said.

"It gave me—us," Fielding looked at Adelaide, "the notion to share this venture with all of you. You would all be partners and share in the profits. You may be involved as little or as much as you wish. Your profit will equal your contribution, naturally."

"What is the stumbling-block?" Philip asked, knowing no one else probably would.

Fielding shook his head. "There is none. I have extended the same invitation to Matthias, Colin, and Kitty, for her share as Peter's widow. Since I am but an honorary member of the brethren, Tobin, the offer also extends to you."

Tobin's eyes widened with surprise, but he said nothing.

"For now, my business is with Wellington and the army. It is an interesting proposition, however, and one I will consider," Philip said, not wishing to be driven into a corner. Adelaide had already given him much to consider.

James agreed he would also think on the proposal.

"That is all I can ask. The offer will always be open."

AMELIA CAME DOWNSTAIRS EARLY, determined to speak with Captain Elliot. However, when she made it to the breakfast parlour, there was already a large gathering. The surprise must have registered on her face.

"Good morning, Lady Amelia. Soldiers awake at an early hour," he said as the gentlemen stood for her entrance. Captain Elliot, Waverley, Mr. Fielding, Captain Frome and Tobin were all present around the round table in the square room, richly hued in puce and gold.

"This is early," she replied and glanced at the clock which indicating five past ten.

The gentlemen laughed as she took a seat and they resumed their places.

"Coffee?" Captain Elliot offered.

"Yes, please." She smiled at him sweetly. She had resolved, during the sleepless night she had endured, to put aside her absurd infatuation with him and try to see him for who he was. It was not fair for her to hold a grudge against him when she had created his character in her mind. "What have I missed? Adelaide!" she then exclaimed, seeing her friend across the table. "What a lovely surprise. But of course you are here to see your brother."

"Fielding was kind enough to bring me here."

"Against my better judgement," he said, looking at her fondly.

Captain Elliot cleared his throat. "I was thinking of taking a stroll along the Seine, if anyone would care to join me? Lady Amelia?"

"That sounds lovely, thank you. I would also love to see some of the paintings at the Louvre," she added.

A decided twinkle in his eye, Captain Elliot raised his eyebrows while the other gentlemen groaned and made their excuses.

"I would also love to see the fine arts Paris has to offer, my dear," Adelaide said to her husband, "and I would not object to trying some of the famous pastries here, either," she added.

"My son is craving sweetmeats already?" Fielding laughed. "As you wish."

"Let us meet at noon once it is a bit warmer," Philip suggested.

Amelia sipped her coffee in silence as the gentlemen, and then the Fielding couple, departed one by one. She was left alone with Captain Elliot, who seemed content to let her drink her coffee in peace. While unexpected, it was a charming trait in a gentleman, she noted to herself.

When she set her cup down, he finally spoke. "Would you like another?"

"Yes, I should, sir, but you need not delay speaking, as you have until the first cup is finished." She smiled and he smiled back. There was no flirtatiousness, but a genuine look of shared amusement. Perhaps they could carry out this operation as friends. He was a real person, not the fictitious, romantic hero she had made him out to be. She felt ashamed and it must have shown on her face.

"Why the frown?" he asked as he placed another dainty white porcelain cup of coffee in front of her. "I much prefer the smile."

"It is nothing." She placed the requested smile on her face and looked up from the coffee. "I was thinking of something silly and realized how wrong I was about a matter connected. It is of no consequence."

"Very well. Have you made a decision? Waverley told me you have opened the door for an invitation to the fortress for me."

"I have," she said, not without a certain amount of pride. "My aunt thinks I am indulging in a flirtation with you. She thinks my mind would be elsewhere if you were not in attendance."

"Well done, Lady Amelia. Our outing today will help cement that idea, then. Only Wellington, Waverley and your sister know the truth."

"What of Adelaide? I would not wish to keep anything from her."

"Nor I, but they must return to England, and the fewer people who know, the better. I will not lie if she asks."

"What about our outing today?

"It will be exactly as it appears: two friends enjoying a pleasant afternoon together."

Amelia relaxed. She would be far more comfortable with Adelaide present.

"I will see you at noon," she said, and finishing her coffee, left the room and made her way upstairs.

When she returned, an open landau was waiting to take them around the city, and Captain Elliot was already waiting when she arrived downstairs.

"Punctual this time, I see. Very well done." He made a gesture of checking his watch and snapping it shut.

"Do not become accustomed to it," she warned. "I was already dressed for the day. I only needed my bonnet, pelisse and gloves." She looked around. "Where are Mr. and Mrs. Fielding?"

"Unfortunately, my sister is feeling unwell, but assures me it will pass soon. They will join us at the museum."

Amelia tried not to show her disappointment. "Are they expecting a happy event, then?"

"Indeed they are."

"I must proffer my congratulations to them. It appears as if we will both become an aunt and an uncle at about the same time."

"It seems our families are full of domestic bliss." He held out his arm. "Shall we? Would you prefer to walk or drive? I ordered the carriage because of Adelaide's condition, but we may leave it if you wish."

"I think seeing Paris on foot is more romantic, although I would hardly call the weather pleasant."

He eyed her suspiciously. "It will certainly offer more opportunity to instruct you."

"Instruct me? What do I need to know beyond how to eavesdrop? I am already an expert at that," Amelia said, knowing she was provoking him.

He stopped and abruptly turned her to face him; he looked long and hard into her eyes. She struggled to read what he was thinking in his deep blue eyes, even as her breathing sought to quicken.

After a tense moment, he relaxed and let her go.

"May I ask what you meant by that?" she demanded.

"I had to assure myself," he said as he took her arm and began to stroll out the gates down the avenue as the wind whipped a spray of leaves across their path.

"Assure yourself of what, pray tell?" she asked, lifting her parasol over her shoulder with a snap.

"That you are not as big a fool as you are trying to convince me."

"It works on most men," she replied nonchalantly.

"I imagine it does, but I am trained to detect lies."

She sighed heavily. "How do you want me to behave?"

"When you are with me, as yourself."

"You flirted outrageously with me when we first met, but that is not who you really are, either."

"Touché. I propose a truce: we be only ourselves."

"No one likes who I really am," she admitted. "I would never be noticed if I behaved as I wished."

"That is coming it too strong. People cannot but notice you."

"What does that mean?" she asked, but he pulled her into a narrow alley before she knew what was happening.

"Pretend to embrace me," he said, seconds before drawing their faces and bodies close using her parasol as a shield.

Amelia trembled with fear, for she could tell he was protecting her from something. He was discreetly watching the street. She tried to relax, which was no small feat with the strength of her laces; a moment later, he released her and stepped back. He put his finger over his lips and she nodded understanding.

He took her hand and pulled her forward. "Look beneath your bonnet across the street."

She adjusted her eyes and found what—or rather, who—he was talking about. Her aunt's man, Lannes, was coming out of a building lined with shops and cafés.

"What am I supposed to see? Something nefarious? I see *ma tante's* man."

"What is he doing?"

"Looking around, maybe for someone," she answered.

"Precisely."

She turned her head and found his close beside hers. She considered him questioningly.

"He is following us," he explained. "He knows he lost us here, so he is waiting for us to re-emerge from one of the shops."

"Oh, good heavens. Why is he following us? How can you be so certain?"

"'Why?' indeed. He has been following us the entire time we have been promenading. He stops when we stop. Come this way."

He took her hand and led her down another narrow alley towards the river. The thrill of being chased caused her pulse to quicken, and she easily followed at his pace, grateful she had chosen half-boots instead of slippers. He hailed a river boat and hired it for a ride. It was a small craft and the oarsman was wrapped in a woollen coat and scarf tied about his neck with a round felt hat low over his ears and eyes. He handed her down then sat opposite her.

"I doubt he will suspect the river," Amelia said appreciatively, pulling her pelisse close to shield herself from the cold air off the water.

Captain Elliot appeared distracted, so she took the opportunity to study him. He was still one of the most handsome men she had ever seen, with his ebony hair and blue eyes which matched his sister's, but there was something different about him now from when she had met him before—some quality of mystery and darkness. She wanted to know what he had been doing and where he had been while he was missing. Now was not the time to ask.

They floated along, past the Tuileries Palace and the Notre Dame, where the river began to turn the boat around the island known as the Ile Saint-Louis, and Captain Elliot spoke.

"Just there is where some of the beheadings of the Revolution took place." He pointed south of the island, where she could see the beginnings of a square with a pool of water.

She shivered. "It has not been so long since the barbarianism took place."

"We are all barbarians inside. We only need the right impetus to bring it out."

"Speak for yourself, sir," she answered brusquely. "I could not harm a rabbit."

"Trust me, I am. I have seen it too many times to deny it exists."

CHAPTER 7

*P*hilip had not expected to be followed. Was he being followed or was the man watching Lady Amelia? It was not just anyone trailing them; he was La Glacier's most trusted lieutenant. Were they just suspicious, or did they know? Of course she would expect they were plotting something, because she was herself. One always had to look over one's shoulder when it came to the enemy. *Always keep your enemies closer.* It was bound to become a game of cat and mouse between Napoleon and Wellington, even if others were acting on their behalf. The spying had been going on covertly throughout the hostilities; now it would be more open, only beneath the pretence of being social discourse.

At least Philip's senses were still on alert enough to recognize another's presence when he had such distraction before him as the fair Lady Amelia.

By the time they arrived at the Louvre, it was far past the hour they had been supposed to meet Fielding and Adelaide. They had therefore returned to the house without the couple's chaperonage, and he was now waiting for his sister to join him for tea. He thought more about the proposition Fielding had made. It seemed he had overreacted when his sister had broached the subject that morning, and it would not be charity—at least not only to him. The offer had been made to all of the brethren who did not wish to continue as half-pay officers once they finished their service with the army. Welston Park was still his. It seemed too good to believe. When this assignment was over, he would inquire of his solicitor what his means truly were. They would never be enough to support someone like Lady Amelia, who was herself an heiress, but perhaps he could live out his days comfortably.

"Every time I see you, you are deep in thought," Adelaide said, having come into the yellow drawing room unnoticed through his reverie.

"There is much to consider and this is a safe place to do it." He smiled at her. She sat down in the yellow damask chair opposite to his, and the butler brought in the tea-tray he had ordered for her arrival.

"How was your outing with Amelia?" she asked. "I am terribly sorry to have disrupted your plans."

"You did nothing of the sort. I hope you were able to enjoy some of Paris and see some of the fine arts?"

"Yes, of course. Fielding would not let me stay out very long, but I did see the Mona Lisa and purchase some fabrics to be made into gowns."

"He must be an uncommonly good husband if he took you shopping for fabrics! Will you be leaving in the morning?" he asked.

"It seems we must. Will you please think on Robert's offer?"

"I will," Philip surprised himself by saying, "but I must complete my duties to the army."

"And Amelia? What of her?" His sister was fishing with a whale harpoon for sardines.

He had hoped she would not ask that question. He wished she had heard nothing, *but then a sister has an uncanny way of discovering such things,* he mused behind a practised bland expression.

"We are friends."

She stared at him in the annoying, knowing way sisters had, clearly not accepting his avowal.

"Would you believe me if I said it was a professional relationship?"

"Philip!" she scolded.

"No, no, you misunderstand." He held up his hands. "I cannot say more, and I am bound in complete secrecy. Suffice to say, she is helping his Grace in a matter of some delicacy, and I am assigned to help her."

"Well, if you are not smitten by her, then you are the first man I have seen to remain impervious."

"She took London by storm, did she?"

"You could say she blew all before her like the strongest gale," Adelaide confirmed. "I will say one thing, though, as a word of caution."

"I am a grown man, sister." Philip did not want to be scolded.

"A sister may still care. I wanted to say, Amelia is not at all as she pretends to be in front of Society. She is a very kind and caring person and I would not wish to see her hurt."

"So your concern is for her, not me?" He laughed.

"Do not be ridiculous. A woman's feelings are different when it comes to forming attachments."

He looked upward in exasperation. "I never thought to be lectured by my little sister."

"You are both important to me and I want what is best for both of you. I shall say no more."

"Lady Amelia is in no danger from me. I should be no more than a flirtation for her, I assure you. When the time comes for her to choose a husband, she will look far beyond mere Captain Philip Elliot."

"I wish you would not speak of yourself—or her—in such a manner. She cares not for such superficialities. She has had every opportunity to make a splendid match."

"Maybe not now, I will grant you, but she will when the lustre has faded."

"Whatever has brought you together, dear brother, there is a reason for it, just as there was a reason I became a governess."

"That never should have happened. If I had not—"

"No, stop!" Adelaide held up her hand. "It was the best thing that could have happened to me."

"You always could see the good in everything."

"The alternative is seeing the bad and where would that leave me?"

"Where I am," he teased.

Later that evening, Amelia received an invitation to join Captain Elliot in the study. It made an interesting change, to be working, in a manner of speaking. Under no circumstances would she be able to do such a thing in London, as a young, unmarried woman. In fact, if word ever got out, her chances of a good marriage would be nil. The taste of adventure was too much to resist, however, and even though she had had the wool removed from her eyes with regards to Captain Elliot, he still intrigued her. Then, of course, there was her aunt. Amelia felt divided in her loyalty, and dearly hoped the investigation would vindicate her aunt of whatever the British government suspected.

Uncertain how she should dress for a summons to the study to discuss her work with Captain Elliot, Amelia considered her wardrobe. What was one to wear to such things? Doubtful he would approve of anything frivolous, she chose a black gown in a subdued style, had her maid dress her hair in a simple knot, and made her way to the study.

When she arrived, Wellington and Waverley were present as well, in addition to Captain Frome, Tobin and Captain Elliot. The gentlemen stood up when she entered. It was intimidating to realize she would be the eyes and ears for this operation, along with these esteemed men who had vast amounts of experience in the army. Seeing them together, in this room, made her question her previous bravado. What if her aunt was killed? She herself could be killed!

"Lady Amelia, at last," Wellington said in his customary brusque manner. "Please come and take a seat. We have much to discuss."

The gentlemen were sitting in the smaller yellow drawing room, a decidedly feminine-looking room sitting in dainty chairs surrounded by gilt and fringe. Had they met in this room for her as opposed to a more masculine smoking room or study?

"Your Grace." Amelia dropped a curtsy to Wellington and nodded towards Waverley before taking her seat.

"Elliot tells me you have made a good start. He has received his invitation to the fortress this afternoon."

"I am happy to be of service, sir," she said, wondering what she was doing.

"Elliot also tells me you were followed. We are not yet certain what that means. It might simply have been Madame trying to see the nature of your association."

Amelia cast a glance at Captain Elliot, who was watching her closely. She tried not to squirm under his gaze and looked around the room at the other gentlemen. Tobin quickly glanced away, but Captain Frome smiled at her as he would have done in the London ballroom. She smiled back.

"On the other hand," Wellington was saying, "they could have decided Elliot is a threat and could be trying to determine what he knows. Therefore, it is of the utmost importance for La Glacier to think Captain Elliot is indispensable to Lady Amelia and that he has aspirations to her hand. He will make a point of announcing his retirement from His Majesty's service and hint at plans for your future together."

Amelia swallowed hard, trying not to outwardly react to this news, even though she knew it was an act. It would not be so awkward had it not been her dream, until recently, to marry him. She could be sophisticated about this.

"Given her dowry, and what a handsome couple you make, it might not be such a bad idea for you, Elliot."

Amelia studied the trimming on her gown and did not comment.

"I will not truly be resigning my commission, Lady Amelia, so you need not concern yourself."

"I am not concerned," she assured him calmly, having outwardly composed herself. She looked at Wellington. "How may I help minimize the threat to Captain Elliot?"

"Keep him out of trouble, my dear."

"I will pretend I did not hear that remark, your Grace," Captain Elliot muttered.

Wellington laughed. "Now, you are not to do anything dangerous, young lady. By having you and your sister at Madame Lisette's estate, it allows me to put my people there, and will make her wonder what I am about."

"What are you about, sir? Games of intellect with my aunt?" she asked boldly.

Someone inhaled loudly but Wellington did not seem to notice.

"Most of war strategy is gaming of sorts. My sources tell me that she is still communicating with Napoleon, and that his army is still loyal to him, not the King. It also appears she is planning to visit him. I am hoping she will reveal more information somehow. Every little detail you hear could matter, even if you think it of little consequence."

"How am I to relay information to you? I assume I will be watched."

"Of course. That is why you are enraptured with Captain Elliot. You can whisper your findings to him in the guise of young lovers."

"I think it would be easier to tell my sister or her husband."

"Perhaps, but the more direct the communication the better. Elliot is my most experienced man and is accustomed to relaying information back to me. He has spent the past year building a system of communication near Étretat."

"Captain Frome and Lieutenant O'Neil will also be nearby, in disguise. Frome will be a fisherman and O'Neil will be making deliveries." It was difficult for Amelia to think of Tobin as Lieutenant O'Neil. Captain Frome inclined his head and winked.

"You have your signal, I am told," Wellington stated, and she demonstrated with her earring. "You are not to go anywhere alone with anyone, apart from Elliot or Waverley, of course."

"I understand," she answered, though beginning to feel trepidation.

"You have a weapon?"

"Is that necessary?" she asked, trying not to panic as the reality of what she was about to do hit her fully.

"Indeed it is. Elliot, see to it she is equipped with one of those daggers that hides in the bodice," Wellington said crisply. He did not flinch at mentioning unmentionables in front of a lady. Amelia's cheeks burned and in that moment she felt like a green girl unused to male society.

"Does everyone understand their assignments?"

"Yes, sir." The gentlemen's answers echoed around the room.

"Excellent. Hopefully, there will be nothing to report and the Duchess and Lady Amelia will have a pleasant family visit. I cannot leave any stone unturned, however. I appreciate your willingness to help your country, Lady Amelia. I know it cannot be easy. Waverley." With a nod to the latter, the Duke also acknowledged his part in the operation.

As the gentlemen dispersed, Amelia rose, walked over to the terrace doors and went outside. She leaned on the iron railing, and looking up into the sky, searched for some sense of clarity in her thoughts. There was no turning back now, and she only hoped she was equal to the task before her.

She felt Captain Elliot's presence beside her but did not look down.

"Can I help?" he asked.

"I do not know. I am afraid I will fail someone, no matter what I do either my country or my family."

"It is natural to be afraid. I remember when I first left home for the army. Granted, I was a wild young buck who felt invincible, and men have a more natural tendency to violence, yet that bravado did not last long. When you first sleep on the cold, hard ground and hear the drums beat the battle cry, you realize this might be the end."

"Does the feeling ever go away?"

"I suppose so, in a way. There is a strange excitement which runs through you before a battle. But when we lost one of our brethren, the fear became reality."

"How awful for you!" Amelia turned and looked at him then. It was the first time Captain Elliot had looked vulnerable and something inside her ached for him.

"I will do my best to protect you, Lady Amelia. I think you are beginning to understand the gravity of the situation, if I correctly read your face just now."

She nodded.

"It is an adventure of sorts, and there is a thrill in the chase, but you must also realize the danger. You must trust me completely. Can you do that?"

"Yes," she whispered, looking into his eyes. They were barely visible in the night, but she felt as though she could see him better than she ever had before. In his vulnerable state he had opened up a new side to her; unfortunately, it was one which was far more attractive than the handsome, flirtatious one she had fallen for when she was a silly girl with fantastical dreams. She would now have to be very careful with her heart.

"Thank you," he said sincerely. "I feel much better hearing you say that. I was not certain you would be able to do so when you first arrived."

"To be frank, Captain, neither was I."

"I cannot protect you if you do not tell me everything, is that understood?" He spoke rather fiercely.

"Understood." She tried not to flinch.

"Now, let us get a good night's sleep. We have a long journey tomorrow and will need all the faculties at our command when we arrive."

She smiled sweetly and he took her arm and led her towards the guest apartments. Not another word was said, and Amelia did not feel comforted. What had she done?

CHAPTER 8

*P*hilip worried all night about Lady Amelia. She was not ready for this assignment. He would have to watch over her more closely than he had thought. At first, he had thought her too flippant for such a task. Now she seemed to appreciate the seriousness of the situation, but would her allegiance to England be strong enough? Something had changed between them, although he could not say precisely what. While he had seen the Amelia his sister had spoken of, he still saw a green girl who might melt under pressure.

He led his horse, Scipio, around to where the carriages were being loaded for the journey.

"Something on yer mind?" Tobin asked as he walked up to Philip, carrying his pack.

"Naturally," he answered.

"I do not envy ye yer task. The lass is a bonnie handful."

"Rarely do I question our commander, but I must admit I cannot like this," Philip responded.

"I must agree with you, there. Lady Amelia has a mind of her own, and I do not think she will tell us everything unless it suits her."

Although Philip had the same reservations, he kept his opinion to himself. "I hope she will do what is right."

"The Duchess, now, she be another story, but she saw what her aunt was capable of, and his Grace willna let her out of his sight," Tobin continued.

"When do you leave?" Philip asked.

"Captain Frome and I are travelling by boat so we doona arrive with ye. I must meet him at the docks."

"Godspeed, Lieutenant."

Tobin saluted and then went on his way to meet the Captain.

Philip tightened the girth and then turned around to see Lady Amelia coming down the steps from the house in a dark blue riding habit. She was splendid. It took him a moment to realize she intended to ride instead of being a passenger inside the carriage.

"Good morning, Captain Elliot," she said, with what seemed to be false cheer. It did not appear she had slept any better than he had. She asked, "Or should I call you something else now that you have resigned your commission?"

"Captain Elliot is still acceptable," he said, trying to think of how to convince her to ride inside the carriage. "Are you going for a ride before our journey?"

"Now is not the time to be ridiculous," she snapped. "I have no intention of enduring Waverley and my sister, in such a small space and for that length of time, ever again."

Fair enough, he thought. "What about your safety?" he answered mildly. "There are any number of hazards I cannot protect you from in the open. France is not England, and has her fair share of troubles."

"There is nothing you can say to convince me to ride inside that carriage. Perhaps I will feel differently after a few hours, but I need to clear my head." Her eyes pleaded with him just as Waverley and the Duchess joined them.

Philip glanced at his friend. He shrugged his shoulders as if to say he would get no help from that quarter.

A groom brought out one of Wellington's hunters, one known to be a lively stepper.

"I hope you know how to ride; that horse is only second to Copenhagen in his particularity with respect to his rider."

"We understand each other, do we not, Elmore?" she cooed to the horse.

She reached up to rub the horse's nose and planted a kiss straight between its eyes. The horse nuzzled up to her and Philip wanted to scream. That horse had thrown him off more than once, and he was a consummate horseman! Perhaps he was being unjustly cross, but he did not want to spend the whole journey playing nursemaid to Lady Amelia. He needed to clear his head as well!

Waverley helped the Duchess into the black travelling carriage-and-six and Lady Amelia stood where she was, looking expectantly at Philip. Closing his eyes for a moment, he resigned himself to the courtesy and gave her a boost into the saddle.

The carriages began to roll through the courtyard, on their way to Étretat. Philip held his hand out, indicating for Lady Amelia to lead. They made their way slowly through the streets of Paris without a word and as they rode, he tried to swallow his bile. There was little he could do about Lady Amelia now. He allowed himself to grumble until they reached the countryside; by then, he had mostly accepted the hand he had been dealt. Looking around, now that there was some space, he dearly wanted to give his horse its head. There were rolling hills of farmland now yellow and brown during the fallow season. The day was clear and cold, bringing roses to Lady Amelia's cheeks. She was either absorbed in her own thoughts, or she was ignoring him as her eyes were trained straight ahead. It was acceptable to him either way. He pulled up alongside the carriage and spoke to the Duke.

"Where would you care to stop? I should like to ride on a bit and scout the area."

The Duchess was looking rather green, and suddenly he sympathized with Lady Amelia. The Duke reached up and tapped on the roof of the carriage and Philip was barely able to get out of the way before the Duchess exited the carriage to be sick.

Waverley was hovering solicitously over his wife, and Philip felt very much the intruder. He stood back quietly and waited, turning his back so that the Duchess could have privacy.

When she was cleaned up, the Duke spoke. "We will stop for the night at Aubergenville. Go on ahead and take Amelia with you."

Philip looked around, but Amelia was nowhere to be seen.

"Heaven help me," Philip muttered. "Are you certain you do not want us to stay?"

"Please go on," the Duchess insisted, dabbing her lips with a silk handkerchief.

"Very well," he agreed with more obvious relief that he should have. "Now, where is my charge?" he asked himself sarcastically as he mounted Scipio and began searching.

"Did anyone see which way Lady Amelia went?" he asked the servants who were waiting.

The coachman pointed on ahead and Philip tipped his hat. "I am going to kill her before the day is over," he growled under his breath, turning his horse to follow her. Fortunately for his temper, he had only gone a few hundred feet when he saw her horse grazing at the side of the road. Amelia was emerging from the trees and smiled at him sweetly.

He could not help but scowl at her. "What do you think you are doing?

"A gentleman should never ask a lady that when she had need to use the necessary."

"We are no longer gentleman and lady. Do you realize what could have happened to you?"

"It has only been a few minutes!" she protested.

"We are on our own now, and you will not go off again without me. Do you understand? Or I will tie you up and take you back to the carriage."

"You would not dare!" She set her hands on her hips and glared at him with indignation and colour mounting her cheeks.

"I most certainly would." He jumped down from his horse and stood toe to toe with her, looking down into her mulish, beautiful face. She turned her back on him and crossed her arms.

"Stop treating me like a child," she snapped.

That was a mistake.

Reaching around her, he grabbed her hands and pulled them behind her back, dragging her against him.

"This is not child's play, Amelia. You will agree to follow my orders, or you go back now."

He thought she would refuse. It felt a full five minutes before she answered.

"Very well," she said in a begrudging tone.

"Last night you promised to trust me."

"This is not about trust, it is about control."

"Safety," Philip corrected. "It is about keeping us both safe."

"Will you let me go, now?"

He released her and her scent of violets wafted through the air. She stormed over to her horse and untied it, trying to mount it herself, but she was petite and the horse was not. He stood back and watched with amusement.

"Are you going to be a gentleman and help me, or not? Oh, my apologies. For a moment I forgot that we are no longer a lady and a gentleman."

He watched as she searched for something to use as a mounting block. Finally, she gave up. "Will you assist me, please?"

"Manners at last. Certainly I will help, *mademoiselle*."

He boosted her into the saddle, then mounted his own horse.

"Are you trying to make me hate you?" she asked.

"Not at all. I am trying to let you comprehend that you cannot do this alone. We are partners, like it or not, and independence has no part in this relationship."

Just then, Philip heard something in the trees and his senses immediately went on high alert. He saw her open her mouth to argue further, but he hushed her with a look of warning which, thank God, she understood.

"Start riding now," he commanded quietly, grateful she had obeyed when it mattered.

They rode fast, and pushed their cattle as hard as they dared. He had to give Lady Amelia credit for one thing, at least: she could ride.

He had looked over his shoulder many times, but could not detect anyone following them.

At length, he drew rein. "I think we have lost them."

"I should certainly think so," she said with all of the hauteur of someone who had been raised in the saddle. "What gave you warning?"

"A rustle in the trees."

"It was probably a deer," she said dismissively.

"It could have been someone following us or a highwayman…even if it was an animal, I would not want to defend myself against a wild boar."

"Shall we let the horses rest?" she asked as she dismounted and opened one of the saddle bags, pulling out a blanket.

"An excellent notion. There looks to be some water over there." They dismounted and walked on until they came to a stream. Philip led the horses down a shallow bank to drink.

When he turned around Lady Amelia was setting up a blanket and opening a satchel with a canteen and food.

"What are you doing?"

"Resting?" she asked as though it were obvious.

"We are not on a leisurely afternoon outing. We must take precautions, not merely indulge in a picnic out in the open as though in Richmond Park!"

"We must eat, and we are not 'out in the open' as you put it. We are near a stream, surrounded by trees. Do you care for an apple?" She held up a bright pink piece of fruit, offering it to him with total innocence.

"You will be the death of me," he said. Accepting the fruit, he tore into it in frustration.

She laughed and bit into her own piece. He had to admire her pluck, but why did *he* have to be the one responsible for her?

THIS MAN WAS INFURIATING! The devilish side of Amelia was enjoying taunting him, but while she was afraid she may have pushed him too far, she could not seem to help herself.

"I think you are overly skittish."

"I think you are overly naïve."

"The war is over and Napoleon is happily ruling Elba," she argued.

"You have no idea what you are talking about. Someone like Napoleon will never be content to be under guard, even if his captivity is a farce."

"Even so, why would we be a threat?"

"Because there is unrest and the people are not loyal to King Louis. There are meetings happening in secret all over France, where the good citizens plot to overthrow him again. We can trust no one."

"I still do not see why two young lovers travelling to a country house party would cause any alarm," she said. She delicately licked at some juice dripping from the corner of her mouth.

"My dear Amelia," he said in a different tone, moving closer. The change in his demeanour made her wary.

"I hope this invitation is as innocent as you seem to believe, but I think your aunt is, at this moment, plotting his escape, and I intend to discover precisely how she plans to do it."

Amelia's attention was piqued. "So that is what this is really about. It is much clearer to me now. Why did everyone not tell me from the start?"

"Perhaps they assumed you would deduce as much."

"That was unkind," she scolded as she threw her apple core at him, which he caught and tossed to one of the horses.

"Do you think they will harm us to keep us from discovering their plan?"

"Quite possibly."

"At least I am no longer searching for arbitrary information."

"I do not mean to say there could not be something else to discover." He stood and brushed down his breeches then held out a hand to help her up. "Shall we continue? The Duke and Duchess will catch up to us if we stay any longer."

"I consider that highly unlikely. I thought we would never reach

Paris once we arrived in port," she said, reaching down to gather the blanket and fold it. Philip went to fetch the horses from the bank where they were grazing.

When he returned, he was creeping slowly, a look of alarm on his face as his hand went to his belt.

"What..." she began to ask, just as a hand covered her screams.

"Do not hurt the girl," a second, authoritative voice commanded.

Amelia stared in terror at Philip, who looked ready to strike if necessary.

"May I help you?" he asked. "We are merely *deux amants* on our way to visit friends and family near Le Havre."

"I know who you are," the man spat.

"Then what do you want from us?"

Amelia wished the one holding her would take his hand away from her face before she gagged from the smell of rotten onions pressing against her.

"I want you to promise to leave France and cease your interest in Madame Lisette."

"Madame is my betrothed's aunt. We are come on a family visit, nothing more."

Amelia tried to speak but the man's callused palm muffled her words.

"You are a British soldier, *non?*"

"Not any longer, *m'sieur*. I am only a mister wooing my future bride." Philip was creeping closer as he spoke.

"Stay back or I hurt the lady."

"You would not wish to anger Madame. We are going to the fortress at her expressed invitation."

The man paused and looked to the second man, then with obvious reluctance released Amelia. "Very well, but we will be keeping a close eye on you."

As soon as she was free, Philip raised his fist and knocked the man out and released a knife into the second as he came forward to defend his partner. Philip was ready.

"Quick, get the rope out of my bag," he ordered.

Amelia fetched him the rope, and while he worked, binding one man to a tree, the other began to stir and try to regain his feet.

Amelia panicked, and reached for the small dagger within her bodice, thrusting it into him before he could advance any farther.

The older man groaned and fell face forward to the ground.

"I killed him!" The horses objected to her screeching and Scipio reared, bringing his forelegs down upon the man, making a horrific crushing sound.

"If you did not, Scipio did."

Philip calmed the horses and commanded them to stand. "Hold them back," he told Amelia as he checked the downed man for life.

He looked concerned, since it was obvious the man was dead. He pulled her dagger from the body and wiped it clean before handing it back to her.

She took it as though it contained the plague, and did not want it back. "What do we do with him?"

"I think we had better make it appear the two of them had an altercation. Gather our things so we can leave as soon as I am ready."

Amelia felt sick. She had never harmed anything in her life and now she had killed a man! Captain Elliot untied the ropes with which he had just bound the first offender to the tree and placed him near the body of the attacker.

"I hit him hard enough that he will wonder what happened when he wakes. Now, we must get as far away from here as we can. We will follow the river for a while so we are not seen anywhere near this place."

Amelia followed, not saying a word, and wondering how she would be able to live with herself after committing such a horrid act.

"Do not be so hard on yourself," Captain Elliot said gently. "The first time you see a man die...alters you."

Amelia let out the sob she was trying to hold back. "How do you live with yourself?"

"You do not have a choice," he answered, the infuriating man. "You were very brave and thought quickly when under attack."

"I would beg to differ. If I had not plunged a dagger into him, he would be alive!"

"You poor girl. Your dagger did not kill him, the horse did."

Amelia burst into tears, then. "So my screeches were more effective than my weapon?"

"The horse landed on his neck and broke it, although I am certain he would have bled to death from your stab wound if Scipio had not helped."

"This is ludicrous."

"The conversation is, but the threat is not. Hopefully, you will believe me now."

Amelia was tempted to thrust her dagger into him, but at least she had stopped crying.

CHAPTER 9

*T*he rest of the journey was uneventful, thank goodness. They followed alongside the Duke and Duchess' carriage for the remainder, which kept them safe from attacks and Philip free of the exchanges with Lady Amelia, which had become more intimate than Philip had intended. When on active service, it was best to keep relationships professional and at a distance. He had no idea how he was going to accomplish that when they had to pretend to be considering marriage.

As they climbed the long, steep path up to the fortress, Philip saw the guards as they passed. They were supposed to be well hidden, but it was one of the things he had quickly discovered during his time reconnoitring the fortress. He knew the hours when the guards changed and he knew there were eight of them, spread from the bottom to the top. After the cavalcade passed through the gate, and the grooms came out to take the horses, Philip knew he had to be very careful not to portray any of *Monsieur Lefebre's* particular characteristics. Superior British mannerisms were the order of the day, he reminded himself.

"*Bienvenue chez moi*," La Glacier said as she came out to greet them dressed in her usual white. Today it was a simple muslin day dress and it made her look more youthful and vulnerable, Philip decided, as he considered her.

"I hope you do not mind, this will only be a small family affair. I do not hold grand entertainment at this, my true home."

"No entertainment is necessary," the Duchess reassured her. "A nice rest in these beautiful surroundings will be very welcome indeed."

Philip knew there were many, many people down beneath the house, in a vast network of prison cells and rooms, but he was not about to mention it. He had waited so long to have access to the castle interior and now his chance had arrived, he was itching to explore.

La Glacier led them inside, and it was nothing like he had expected. Once they passed through the white marble entrance hall, the fortress felt very similar to the house he had grown up in. The little party walked past several rooms, the doors of which were closed, until La Glacier led them into a private saloon where there were comfortable, worn sofas and chairs, books strewn about for pleasure reading and a chessboard.

The suspicious side of Philip wondered if it was all an act to defray their attention from her work for Napoleon, yet it did not feel false. Philip was frustrated. He did not want to think kindly of her, and he knew it would tug at Lady Amelia's feelings. Feelings were dangerous when you were spying.

He watched as their host showed her nieces the view over the cliffs to the ocean. There was a perfect seat with cushions where a person could get lost watching the waves, or even reading. One day, perhaps...

"Please help yourself to any of the books you like. My servants await your pleasure."

"*Merci, Tante,*" Amelia was saying. Waverley was standing back, also observing. Philip wondered what his thoughts were on the situation. He knew there had to be places for eavesdropping, but were there any to be found in the private apartments?

When there was a pause in the conversation between the ladies, Philip spoke up. "Is there any way down to the beach from here," he asked, "for walking along the water?" He smiled at Amelia, hoping La Glacier might think his intentions were romantic.

"But of course," she answered. "I will show you the path when we pass through the courtyard."

Philip knew she suspected him, but precisely how much, he could not say.

"Captain Elliot has resigned his commission, *Tante*," Amelia said.

"Has he, indeed?" The woman cast him a sideways glance.

"With the war now over, there is little for me to do here. In fact, I have some business opportunities awaiting me in England, and my estate needs to be overseen."

"I was unaware you had an estate. That is happy news." She looked approvingly at Amelia. So far, she seemed to be genuine, and Philip wanted to learn more, but this was not the time.

"I am certain you would like to rest from your long journey. I will have my housekeeper show you to your apartments. It may not be what you are used to, but hopefully you will be pleased."

"I am certain it will be lovely," the Duchess said kindly. "The view reminds me of Hawthorne Abbey, although the water here is a brighter blue."

"I did not have the pleasure of visiting my sister there, but my mother told me of its beauty. Shall we meet back here for tea in two hours? I think my chef will not disappoint you." They followed her into a hall where a white marble staircase led to the upper floors and statues filled every niche. This was more as Philip had expected—a sterile feeling and coldness. However, when they passed through to the private chambers, the furnishing felt warmer again. There were rich blue and red colours with lush carpeting, and the wood-panelled walls were lined with family paintings.

A plump, motherly housekeeper joined them, and showed them to their suites of rooms.

Waverley and Philip followed along behind, and an exchanged glance revealed they were both looking for any sort of clue or sign a rebel army existed below—which they knew it did.

Waverley leaned closer and whispered, "She has to know we are looking."

"Of course," Philip agreed. "I am certain she will greatly enjoy toying with us."

"Any sign of how to enter the tunnels leading below?"

"When I came for Tobin, I entered through the caves by boat, and I did not venture beyond the stables or kitchens when I was making deliveries here."

"These are Napoleon's rooms when he visits," the housekeeper said to the Duchess, showing her into a richly decorated apartment.

"She speaks as though he is coming back," Waverley remarked.

"Perhaps we should just ask her," Philip quipped.

"*Monsieur Elliot*, Madame has selected a special room for you. She said you will find what you seek in here." The housekeeper seemed perplexed, but shrugged and opened a door for him.

Waverley gave him a look as he went into his own apartments, indicating they would speak later.

Whatever could she mean? There were peep-holes? There was a door to Lady Amelia's room? Surely not! There were diaries of her plans with the Emperor? He almost laughed aloud at his wild suppositions. At first glance, it was a normal series of chambers—a dressing room, a sitting room, a bedroom. He crept around the room, removing each painting and checking each stone and panel in the wall. Thankfully, he found no holes, but neither had he found a door or secret compartment. He stared around the room, seeking inspiration and his gaze dropped to the red Turkish rug. The floor!

Sure enough, when he rolled back the carpet, there was a trapdoor. It opened easily on its hinges, and a narrow set of steps led downwards inside the chimney breast.

"The cat strikes first, it seems, but why? Is she baiting me?" He paced around the room, debating what to do. "I am here as her guest, so she cannot throw me in the dungeon—not if she wants to please her niece." He turned another circle, weighing his options. "Either she has nothing to hide, or she does not care, although she has had time to remove any evidence. No. I refuse to be prey... and yet is it not a trap I am considering?" Indeed, he could not resist looking and began to creep down the stone steps one by one.

The stairs wound around and around for several storeys. At length, he surmised that he was nearing the tunnels and the sea, for the smell of salt and damp grew stronger, and the air grew chill. He tried several doors as he passed them, but none opened until he reached the bottom. It creaked loudly as he opened it, and he suspected it led to the tunnel where he had been before, to negotiate Tobin's release. Instead, there was a large study with a fire roaring in a blackened iron grate, and Madame was sitting behind a heavy desk.

"You have come at last," she said, standing and walking around to the front and then leaning against the desk.

"How could I refuse such an invitation?"

"I have no secrets to hide from you. You know I am French, and a supporter of the Emperor. My question is, are you hiding something from me, or my niece? You see, being the matriarch of her family now, it is my responsibility to protect her. I am partial to military men myself, but they do not usually make good husbands."

"I have resigned my commission."

"Yet you are here."

"What can I say? You dangled the forbidden fruit in front of me. This fortress is fascinating and I have been here before."

"I no longer harbour prisoners or spies here, Captain Elliot, if that is what you suspect. There was a time I did what was needful for my country."

"And I for mine."

She inclined her head. "So we need not be enemies. We both care for my niece, so we may find some mutual interests in her."

Philip knew she was not telling the truth. Had he not heard her plotting with his own ears, however, he might have been convinced.

"We both want what is best for her."

"Lady Amelia will come to no harm at my hands.

"See that she does not."

~

THE NEXT MORNING, after they had broken their fast, Madame invited the ladies to join them in her boudoir. When Amelia and Meg arrived, she was sitting on a pale, pink sofa doing some needlework. For a moment, Amelia thought her aunt was her mother and it took her a moment to recover and compose herself.

"*Bonjour, mes nieces.* I am glad you could join me. This is how I spend most of my mornings."

"I have never had the patience for needlework," Amelia admitted. "Meg, however, is a dab hand at it."

"Amelia is excellent at painting when her nose is not in a book," Meg added with a sly look at her sister.

"I shall have my maid procure some painting supplies for you. There are many beautiful views to be captured here," her aunt said. "Please enjoy some sewing if you like." She indicated a basket on the floor near her chair.

"I would like that, thank you."

Meg picked up some sewing from their aunt's basket and began a pattern. Amelia sat on the window seat overlooking the ocean and was content to watch the waves crash against the rocks below.

"You are not looking well, *ma chérie.* Can I call for something?" their aunt asked Meg.

"It happens every morning," Meg admitted. "If you will excuse me, my maid will aid me."

"But of course. It will pass in a few weeks, I think."

Meg hurried from the room, and Amelia exchanged sympathetic glances with her aunt.

"I wonder that the Duke let her travel in her condition," her aunt said with a shake of her head.

"She would not be kept behind. The truth is, I needed to leave England for a while."

"Troubles with men?" Her aunt glanced up from her stitching.

"Yes," Amelia said meekly. "I could not bring myself to accept any of my suitors, and one of them tried to force my hand."

"I am glad you did not settle for something you could not be happy with." She paused for a moment before asking astutely, "Was it because of Captain Elliot?" Her gaze was far too perceptive.

Amelia blushed despite herself. There was no harm in admitting the truth, she thought, since she and Philip were pretending to be enamoured of one another.

"Forgive me, my dear. I have no right to pry. Even though you have only just met me, I feel a connection to you through your mother. Margaret reminds me of her a good deal, but you remind me of myself."

"Do not apologize. I too, feel a connection, and I miss her so very much."

"One of the hardest things ever to happen to me was to be separated from her. We kept in touch a little by letter and through our mother, but it was not the same once your mama married and left for England." She paused again. "I will always feel responsible for your parents' death. Each and every day it weighs heavily upon me."

"You did not order Hawthorne to kill them. That was his derangement, not yours."

"True," she said softly and stared out of the window past Amelia into the distance for a while. Clearly, she was lost in her thoughts. Amelia gave her the courtesy of privacy and waited.

"I am grateful you have come to me," her aunt said at last.

Amelia turned to look at her, and smiling, reached out her hand towards the other woman. "I am grateful too."

"I may not be your mother, but if you need advice, please ask. Your beauty is both a blessing and a curse, I know. Yet you have one thing I did not—wealth. It is difficult to know whether people desire you for yourself. I used to think I needed to be who they expected, instead of what made me happy."

Amelia felt a lump of emotion rise in her throat. That was exactly how she felt.

"Your mother and sister possess a quiet sort of beauty that attracts the right type of man. You and I are more complicated creatures. We long for adventure, but there are times when we need to be alone and have quiet."

"Yes, I feel guilty and torn at times," Amelia agreed.

"I only say this because I made some very poor choices at your age. Your father was a wonderful man, but I would have been bored to insanity living the life your mother did."

On reflection, Amelia thought perhaps she would have been *ennui* as well, and that was why she could not marry any of the men who had offered for her.

"I see you understand me," her aunt said with a sympathetic smile. "However, I did not find the man who could offer me both worlds, and never found one to make my heart sing."

Amelia's heart sped up. Those were the exact words she had used before to describe Captain Elliot. It was uncanny.

"Therefore you chose to live for a cause? Forgive me if I speak out of turn; I heard certain rumours before I left England, you see," Amelia confessed.

"You may ask me anything you wish. I would rather tell you myself. I did not consciously choose to live for a cause when I was young. I was still searching for true love, I think. My choices soon became limited and I did the best I could at the time. Sadly, it meant separation from your mother and her family."

"What do you think I should do? Go back to England and settle for one of the respectable gentleman who offered for me?"

"Not when I see the way you look at Captain Elliot. Even though we may be on different political sides, I do think he is an honourable man. Whether he is the man for you remains to be seen, but when your heart longs for one person, it would be unfair to commit yourself to another."

"It is hard for the head to overrule the heart. I have been trying."

"It is difficult to see through emotions at your age, and much of marriage is simply luck. I only hope you find happiness."

"You have done well for yourself despite your mistakes," Amelia said daringly, glancing around the room with the wall of glass looking out over the ocean.

"I suppose I have in terms of the manner in which I live. It depends on what makes you happy. I have done the best I could with the decisions I made. It does not mean I would do the same again."

A knock on the door interrupted their tête-à-tête, and Amelia recognized the man who entered as the one from the party in Paris and from her walk with Philip.

Lannes came forward and whispered something to her aunt. Amelia strained to overhear without appearing obvious, but could only make out a few snippets of the hasty conversation.

"...is here."

"What?" she asked angrily.

"He insists on speaking with you."

"I told them I did not wish to be disturbed while my family is here."

"He said it is of the utmost urgency. I bade him wait in your office below."

Her aunt stood up. "Forgive me, Amelia. There is some business I cannot neglect. Perhaps you may find your beau and walk along the beach. It promises to be a beautiful day." She smiled at her and exited the room with her henchman.

Amelia knew she needed to find Philip and report what she had just heard. It could be innocent and nothing more than estate business, but it could be important. She did not wish to tattle on her aunt, who seemed to genuinely care about her and Meg, but she needed to know for more than just her country. She needed to know for herself.

CHAPTER 10

*P*hilip found Waverley in the billiards room practising some shots.

"Mind if I join you?" he asked.

"Please do. Meg is not feeling well, so I thought I would let her rest."

"It is a tough business, growing a child. I am thankful I do not have to do it."

"I think I would rather have the duty myself than watch my wife do it," Waverley said frankly. "Have you any news? The room is clear. I checked it when I arrived. I have been waiting to see what the housekeeper meant by her remarks yesterday."

"There was a secret passageway in my floor that led to the tunnels below. To Madame's office, in fact, where she was waiting to speak with me," Philip said as he hit one of the balls, knocking it into a pocket.

"She was there waiting? Why would she do such a thing?" Waverley asked.

"To prove she is not afraid of us. She said as much."

Waverley began to say more and Philip held a finger over his mouth. Even though Waverley had checked the room, it did not mean they should speak freely about everything. He nodded to indicate his understanding. It was baffling.

"She does seem genuine in her affection for the Duchess and Lady Amelia, which I applaud. She was adamant she is no longer holding prisoners or participating in government activities here."

Waverley was silent as he lined up his shot and hit his cue ball into its target. "Do you have any suggestions? Or do we amuse ourselves with frivolous games and over-indulge in good food and wine?"

"Growing complacent is what she wishes us to do. Perhaps we will find nothing here, but I will not relax my quest." He spoke just above a whisper.

Waverley hit one of his balls into the pocket.

"Nice shot." Philip applauded as there was a knock on the door. He was standing nearby, so he opened it to find Lady Amelia waiting patiently.

"Good afternoon, my lady." He clicked his heels together in greeting.

"Good afternoon, Captain Elliot," she replied. "Waverley," she greeted the Duke as she came into the room. She was dressed for the outdoors in an emerald green velvet pelisse and a matching gathered bonnet.

"Do you think I might impose on you to accompany me on a walk down to the beach?" She looked at him meaningfully, as if urging him on.

"A walk sounds delightful. Allow me a moment to fetch my hat."

"Would you care for company, or is this a romantic tryst?" Waverley teased.

"You may join us if you wish, but I saw my sister emerge from her chamber a few minutes ago and she was looking as well as I have seen her since we left England."

"Say no more," Waverley said, moving towards the door. "Enjoy your walk."

"I will wait for you in the courtyard," she said to Philip and he made haste to get his hat. Amelia admired the umbrella-shaped pine trees surrounding the courtyard as she waited, since a layer of fog had rolled in and was covering the view to the ocean.

They were soon on their way down the stone staircase which led down the cliff from the courtyard to the water. Neither said a word until they had reached a viewing gallery where the steps forked.

"Has something happened?" he asked.

"I do not know, but you said to report everything."

"I did." He nodded encouragingly.

"I was having a pleasant morning conversing with my aunt, and it felt very normal."

"And then?"

"And then her man, the same one from her party, who led her away, came in and whispered to her. She seemed quite irritated to have been disturbed, but she left with him."

"Could you hear anything they said?" He tried not to grow excited. It was early yet.

"Very little, I am afraid. Merely that someone was here to see her and it was urgent."

"We must make haste," he said, taking her hand and pulling her forward.

"Where are we going? We cannot walk in on their meeting!" she insisted, trying to hold her ground.

"We can try to listen. If we are caught, we are out on an afternoon stroll. I need to know who is here."

She said nothing, but stopped resisting. He hoped he could negotiate to the cave opening then on to where La Glacier's office was from his memory of the day before. He followed the southward path down to the shore, holding Amelia's hand firmly. To his annoyance, it ended and there were only boulders leading towards the caves and tunnels he knew to be there.

Unfortunately, it did not seem there was a way to get there without crossing some water. The tide was in, and it was too high for them to negotiate safely and without swimming. He cursed under his breath.

"What is it?" she asked.

"See that cave over there? That is where we need to be."

"Oh, dear." She looked across the white chalk cliff with sharp horizontal stripes to where a cave's entrance was protected by boulders with the tide in.

"My sentiments also, if said in a polite way," he retorted.

"Are you going to swim over there?"

"The thought was crossing my mind, though I do not relish the ice bath. However, I do not wish to leave you here with the tide high."

"I am quite capable of waiting here alone." She huffed with indignation. "I will return to higher ground if the water comes close."

"Very well, then; turn around."

She did as directed and he loosened his neckcloth; then they heard voices.

"Quiet," he commanded in a whisper, at the same time pulling her against the rocks of the cliff face.

Voices echoed towards them; could they really be so fortunate?

"Get in the boat, and do not return until you receive word from me. You cannot risk being seen here again." Resounded off the cave walls through the fog, La Glacier's voice was harsh.

Amelia sucked in her breath.

"Forgive me, Madame, I thought you would wish to know."

"The death is unfortunate, but I could have been informed by post."

"Very well; everything is still on schedule?"

"Yes, the family visit is temporary, but very important to me. We will resume as soon as they leave. *Bonjour, Pierre.*"

The meeting must have ended, for though he strained to do so, he heard nothing more.

"She lied to me," he said. "I knew she was lying, of course, but she said she was no longer carrying out government activities from the fortress."

"Maybe she is doing something else." Lady Amelia tried to defend her aunt.

"You are remarkably naïve. I overheard her organizing the rebel army at her underground meeting in Paris."

"You think she is starting another uprising?"

"I think she is keeping the army prepared for her emperor's return."

Amelia's face fell. "If so, there would be further war between our nations."

"Do not lose heart, my dear." He patted her cheek like he would a small child. She glared at him, which was his intention. When she was irritated she forgot to be sad.

"Do you think the visitor was reporting the man I killed?"

"Most likely," Philip agreed.

"Does she know it was us?"

"Most likely. We were defending ourselves, and I would be happy to tell her so. Now we must act as if we are spending a leisurely afternoon together. It would not surprise me if there was a guard watching us at this very moment."

"Guards?" she asked, with what appeared to be abhorrence.

Philip tried to keep the mockery from his face. "Yes, my dear, guards. They are posted all about the fortress. I can show them to you if you wish. What I do not know, is whether we can be seen from this angle through the fog." He looked around and out over the water. "Do you see that boat over there?"

She held up her hand to shield her eyes and squinted. "Yes, I believe I see a fishing boat."

"That would be our good Captain Frome."

"I see another boat further over there," she said, pointing.

"That could be a fishing boat, or one of her guards. Captain Frome will know and report to me later."

He took her hand and kissed her on the cheek.

"Do you see someone?"

"No, but that is for anyone who may be watching. I imagine, as we speak, Captain Frome can see us through his spyglass."

She smiled and gave a little wave. "Just in case," she said with a coy grin, and batted her eyelashes for good measure.

"Have mercy, my lady. Please tell me you did not behave in such a manner in London?"

She slapped him on the sleeve. "I am only jesting. Must you be such an oaf?"

"Promise me, if this all goes very wrong, you will never take up the stage," he responded, egging her on.

"How does your sister tolerate you?"

"I will have you know, my sister thinks I am the best of brothers."

"May we return to the house, now?"

"I have no objection, if you wish to leave. I must do some more scouting. I have never had the opportunity from this angle, and we need to be prepared for anything."

"I will not leave if you think there is work to be done. How may I help?"

"You do not happen to have a drawing-book, do you?"

"I can obtain one. My aunt offered to provide me with paints."

"Are you an artist?" He looked back, surprised.

"What gently bred woman is not skilled with a brush?"

"Clearly, you have not seen Adelaide's efforts. Very well. Tomorrow we will return and you can draw a map for me."

They began the return journey, and were climbing back over the rocks towards the steps leading to the house when they saw a boat had drawn near to the shore.

"What is he doing coming close in the middle of the day?" Philip asked, growing angry.

"We are about to find out," Amelia remarked.

"We will continue around to the steps; the beach is on the other side of this outcrop."

They climbed back to the fork and took the other path. Lady Amelia did not complain, he noted. She simply lifted up her skirts and kept up with him.

They reached the beach where his adventure had started, months past, and he took Lady Amelia's arm as though they were out for a stroll. They watched the boat come even closer.

"Do you think we can be seen from here?" she asked.

"From certain angles, very likely. The fog is not thick enough."

"Why would he take such a risk?"

"An excellent question." Philip thought that he could see Frome, but they were still too distant.

"Look!" Amelia said. "He is putting something into the water."

Philip saw an object drop, and then the boat continued on its way.

"Continue walking, and act as though we did not notice. It will only draw more attention to it if someone is watching. It will take some time for it to wash ashore. At least the tide is still in."

Philip did not take his eyes from the object, and Lady Amelia walked about along the shore, picking up shells and exclaiming with well-feigned joy at such moments when she saw a crab poke its head out of the sand and scurry away, or a fish jump out of the water. At least she was not missish, he reflected.

Finally, the bottle came close enough for Philip to retrieve it. He waded into the water a few steps and immediately grabbed it, pulling it beneath his coat.

"Shall we return to the house? I think we have had enough sun for today. Your cheeks are quite rosy from the wind."

"We cannot have that, now can we? I might develop some spots!" she said with mock horror.

Philip laughed, forgetting himself. "I already see one, just there," he said, touching her nose and following it with a quick peck, as he might with his sister, except she was not his sister, and it had not been an act.

DINNER THAT NIGHT was an intimate affair, with Meg, Waverley, Captain Elliot, her aunt, that lady's man Lannes, and Amelia herself. Amelia had spent the remainder of the afternoon alone in her apartment, trying to sort through her feelings. It was not an easy task and she was more confused when her maid came to dress her for dinner than she had been when she began trying to think. She could easily envisage becoming fond of her aunt, filling the void left when her mother died. It was much too soon, of course to feel such things, but there had been a connection she could not ignore.

Then, she had heard for herself evidence of her aunt having some sort of activity in the caves below, but it did not prove to her that Lisette was doing anything dreadful against England. As if that was not enough for her poor nerves, Amelia had spent the afternoon alone with Captain Elliot. Most couples did not have the luxury of spending so much time together while they were courting. She had seen the change in him when he had kissed her on the nose. In truth, it was something a brother would do to a sister, but he had not meant to do it and the shock had registered on his face—and left a stamp on her heart. It was too much to be borne.

Now, sitting next to him at dinner, she felt shy and awkward. Her aunt's perceptive gaze would miss nothing, so Amelia had to find a way to perform in this small, intimate setting.

"Did you enjoy your outing today, niece? Your cheeks give you away."

"I did, Aunt. I have not hunted for shells on the beach in years; and the view—I long to capture it on canvas."

"That will be arranged. I would be pleased to own a piece of yours, if you would do me the honour. And you, Captain Elliot? Did you find any treasure?"

"Sadly, only an old bottle washed up by the tide. Alas, there was no secret message inside."

Amelia tried to hide her alarm. It was as though her aunt knew. Had she been watching? She sipped at her *soupe à l'oignon* and studied the participants.

Captain Elliot was smiling at her. Was this all an elaborate game? Amelia wanted to know what had been in that bottle.

"I am certain this beach is full of surprises, if you keep looking."

The servants removed the soup and brought in a *salade niçoise*, a beautiful array of greens, tomatoes, eggs and anchovies.

"This is delicious. I will have to discover your gardener's secrets," Meg said, changing the subject.

"I believe the secret is simply sun, something France has in more abundance than your England," her aunt said. "I am happy we have found something to please you."

Amelia knew Meg did not care for anchovies, so she avoided her gaze and took the opportunity to watch her aunt and the man, Lannes. He was making no secret of examining them.

"I hope everything was in order earlier?" Amelia smiled at Lannes as she spoke. His mien was cool and she barely detected a flicker of reaction in his gaze.

"Perfectly," her aunt answered as she dabbed at the corner of her mouth with a napkin. "Only a business matter that was not nearly as urgent as my steward seemed to think it was." She half-smiled. "I am sure you know how that is, Waverley."

"Yes, of course," he agreed. "What type of business are you in? We are considering joining in a new partnership with one of our army brethren."

"We have begun importing and exporting with the Isle of Elba," her aunt said without hesitation. "They have succulent olives which make excellent oil, and we have superior wine and brandy, of course."

"I am certain your emperor appreciates having luxuries from his home," Captain Elliot said sardonically.

"Everyone appreciates the luxuries of France, *non*? We sell more to England than anywhere else. Speaking of which..." She snapped her fingers and the servants brought out a burgundy wine, then replaced the salad with a fragrant *confit de canard.*

Immediately, Meg covered her nose with her napkin. "Please excuse me," she barely managed to say before hurrying from the room.

Aunt Lissette gave a sympathetic smile. "I will instruct my chef to make something more plain. I do forget."

"There is nothing to apologize for. Thankfully it is a temporary condition." Waverley took a bite of the dish. "This duck is delicious. Please send my compliments to your chef."

She inclined her head and dinner conversation remained innocuous. After the duck, a small dish of chocolate soufflé was served, and Waverley excused himself to discover how Meg was feeling.

"You will forgive me," Aunt Lisette said as the Duke departed. "I must also deal with some business this evening. Captain Elliot will, no doubt, keep you entertained with a walk in the courtyard or a scintil-lating game of chess. I would be *de trop* with only the three of us remaining."

Apparently, Lannes was not considered a person. Amelia was quite certain she did not desire any more time alone with Captain Elliot, but it could not be helped. He stood up as her aunt left the room, and held out his arm to Amelia. "Shall we?"

"Your aunt is toying with us," Captain Elliot said in a low voice once they were alone in the courtyard.

"I am afraid you are correct," Amelia agreed. Walking to the wall, they stood looking out over the vast expanse of ocean. She could hear the waves crashing on to the rocks, and see a few bobbing lights from boats still out in the night. "It does not prove anything, however. I have been desperate to know what message was in the bottle. Will you please share it with me?" she asked in hushed tones.

"Nothing of great import, I am afraid. Frome confirmed our suspi-cions that boats have been coming and going into the caves."

"It could be nothing more than her import and export business," Amelia argued.

"A timely, convenient cover. I will send word to Tobin to have it investigated. In my time living in the village, I have heard nothing of her dealing in spirits, legal or otherwise."

"That is curious. Do you think the villagers would have known? My aunt is very secretive."

"How could they not?"

"I suppose you are correct. I do not know what to believe."

"It is a very clever reason for her to be preparing for a trip to Elba. I know there is something I am missing, I just cannot put my finger on it," he said with a frustrated sigh.

"Even if she were to be doing business with Napoleon, that does not mean she will be successful in helping him escape. Even if he should escape, it does not mean he will lead France again," Amelia pointed out.

"Both are true statements. However, we need to find out what we can."

"What do you propose we do next?"

"You will help me make a map of the fortress and caves. I need to do some exploring."

"Do you intend to search the tunnels?"

"The tunnels, her office, the dungeons, everywhere I can."

"You will get yourself killed! She would have every right to do so for your trespasses."

"Hush, my dear, we are now being watched." He stepped close to her and whispered in her ear, tucking a lock of hair behind it.

"Can you tell who it is?"

"No, but they are too tall to be your aunt or her man. Put your arms around my neck," he ordered.

She did as she was told, but protested. "Is this really necessary?"

"It might save my head later if she thinks I matter to you."

"Very well." Amelia did not like how the closeness made her feel. She did not wish to react to Captain Elliot, and it was difficult to keep her emotions professional when she had never been this close to a man before. She was certain he was watching the guard, and here she was trying not to swoon! It was grossly unfair!

"Why is he not leaving?" Captain Elliot whispered in frustration.

"Perhaps he was ordered to stay, no matter what."

"Beware, I am going to kiss you."

She would remain detached. It was only a touching of lips, after all.

Before she could firm her resolve, his lips were touching hers. She had never been kissed before, and it pained her to admit that this meant nothing. Beyond the tingling sensation she already felt all over, strange things began happening to her insides; she felt both hot and cold.

The hand he placed on her back pulled her closer while his other hand traced circles on her neck. Then it cradled her cheek. Napoleon could have come upon them with a sword, and she would not have noticed.

Seemingly without her volition, her head turned to find a better angle and her lips began to move over his.

"What are you doing, Amelia?" He stepped back. "The guard has left."

If that was not the most lowering thing ever to happen to her, she did not know what was.

"Thank goodness, I was growing exceeding uncomfortable," she said, lifting her chin and heading back into the house and her apartments to hide, knowing she would think of ten far more clever retorts once she was in her room alone.

CHAPTER 11

*P*hilip returned to his room and collapsed on to the bed.

"The lady discomposed you so badly, eh?" a thick Irish brogue asked from the corner. "If I were trying to woo a lass, I would kiss her back."

"How the devil did you get in here?" Philip demanded, remaining on his bed with his hands over his face. The last thing he needed at this moment was to deal with an Irish rogue.

"I told the guards I was your valet."

"I will have to warn La Glacier to tighten her security."

"Whatever takes your fancy. Are ye not going to ask why I am here?"

"I suppose I will need a brandy for this." Philip rose and removed his neckcloth and coat, then went to the cupboard and poured two glasses of the excellent brandy La Glacier had left for her guests.

"How did you get in, truly?" he asked, handing Tobin a glass.

"I walked right in. Captain Frome brought me up to the beach, and after some exploring, I followed the steps that led to the courtyard. It was a lovely conversation you and Lady Amelia were having."

"I should draw your cork for that," Philip snarled.

"Be my guest," Tobin drawled in his thick brogue. "The Madame has quite an operation going underneath this fancy house. If you will recall, I spent some time there."

"Yes, I recall. One might think there would be a mite of gratefulness accorded to your rescuer."

Tobin grunted. "I took it upon myself to visit the cave again."

"Are they not guarded? I confess I have not been able to go down there alone yet."

"Oh, they are guarded, but I remembered their affinity for cards and good drink."

"It was so easy? La Glacier will not be pleased when she discovers them."

"That is their problem. I sent them an entire barrel with her complements. There are no prisoners down there just now."

"She said as much," Philip agreed.

"But there are supplies enough for another war."

"Go on," Philip said cautiously.

"Uniforms, guns, ammunition, swords, canons, rations, tents…"

"Any olives?"

"Eh?" Tobin looked at him askance.

"Never mind. How many men are down there?"

"A dozen?"

"Nice work." He went over to his travelling bag and found some writing supplies. He handed them to him. "Now, draw what you saw under there."

Tobin took the paper and pencil and began making a rough drawing.

While Tobin drew, Philip sat back down and contemplated what it all meant. The rebels were far better prepared than any of them had anticipated. Wellington needed to be apprised immediately. When Tobin had finished, Philip walked to the Irishman's side and looked over his shoulder.

"You are confident in this?"

"These are the areas I saw with me own eyes. I could not say what is beyond here." He pointed to an empty space beyond the office she had taken Philip to.

"Where are you staying?"

"In the village, in your old room." Tobin smirked. "The kitchen maid also seems to prefer Irishmen."

"You have taken up my old post?"

Tobin inclined his head.

"You had best be careful. If La Glacier sees you here, I may not be able to save your neck a second time."

"She will not see me."

"I think you need to deliver this message in person. I do not want it being passed to a runner."

"Who will watch the village?"

"One of the other couriers can stay in your place."

Tobin hesitated.

"That was an order, Lieutenant, not a suggestion. The kitchen maid will still be here when you get back."

"She is a bonnie lass," Tobin said wistfully.

"That she is, and you are welcome to her," Philip agreed. "I will be waiting for your return with bated breath."

Tobin scowled at him and Philip laughed.

"At least I know how to woo the ladies properly."

"I am not wooing Lady Amelia," Philip protested.

"Well, you had better start acting like it at least. That act out there would not have convinced a tree stump."

"I was trying to look out for her guards. Leave me, Lieutenant—and make sure you bring me back some useful news when I see your impertinent face again."

"Aye, Captain." Tobin gave a smart salute and then escaped through the window. Philip looked out after him, and was impressed that he had managed to somehow climb the rocky cliff, for it seemed to fall away beneath the window. Tobin, apparently, was a man of hidden talents.

Philip sat back in an armchair and stared into his glass of brandy, thinking. That La Glacier was preparing an army for war, he had no doubt, but did she intend for Napoleon to lead that army, or someone else? He was glad Tobin was on his way to Wellington, for he did not want his Grace to be caught unawares.

Meanwhile, Philip needed to discover what else was hidden inside of this cliff wall, if anything, and when the army planned to act.

Wellington was sending men to Elba to warn those Navy ships guarding the island to be on alert, but what if it was all a ruse to throw them off the real trail?

Philip removed his boots, and decided he might as well try to get some rest. He turned down his lamp and leaned back in the chair. He was not quite ready to turn in. Perhaps listening to the waves in the dark would calm his mind; his thoughts were racing with information. What was La Glacier about? Something heinous, that was a surety. She must be deliberately trying to lead them astray, and he needed to remain ahead of her.

Then there was a growing problem with the Lady Amelia. He could not ignore his attraction to her, at least to himself. There, he had admitted it. What should he do about that? Falling prey to emotion was the cardinal sin of being a spy, but it was not as if he could control the feeling. Thus far he had been able to control any outward reaction, but for how long could he continue? At all costs, he must avoid physical contact from now on.

When he thought of her sweet lips and her innocent response to him this evening, he could only wish for different circumstances, but there was no possibility of a future between the two of them beyond this assignment. Even if this investigation led to nothing and there was no war forthcoming, he was not an eligible match for her.

He cared enough about her to admit as much. Were he to accept his brother-in-law's offer, he could make much-needed improvements to his estates. The monies forthcoming would not allow him to keep someone like Lady Amelia in gowns and jewels for the life in Town to which she was suited.

There had been times, while sitting watch or riding with messages from place to place, when he'd had time to think of what might have been if he were not a military man. He had surprised even himself by feeling a longing for the life in which he had grown up. That feeling still persisted.

"Maybe one day, Philip, but it will not be with someone like her."

The faster this assignment was over and he could be away from her, the better, he mused, swallowing the final drop of brandy.

A flashing light caught his attention.

"Tobin," Philip muttered under his breath. He jumped up to look out of the window. It was difficult to see through the darkness.

Was Captain Frome out there, somewhere, to help? That there was a boat approaching the fortress, there could be no doubt. The tide was in and he could hear the heave-to of the oars as the crewmen rowed. Somewhere in the distant house a clock chimed one o'clock—in the morning, a time when the household was certain to be abed.

With the danger to be had, why would La Glacier be doing business in the dark of night unless it was of an illegal nature? Perhaps it was the unlawful doings with England La Glacier had alluded to at dinner?

Philip frowned. He needed to find out. He put his boots back on and his coat, then checked to make certain his pistol and knife were in place. He put one booted foot out of the window, reminding himself that Tobin had been able to do it, therefore so should he.

A more foolish sentiment there could not be, he argued with his shrewder self as he looked down below, over the first ledge, and at the water crashing against the rocks. He began to descend slowly, one hand and one foot at a time, until he reached an opening where his foot had nowhere to take hold. He jumped and landed in the mouth of another cave in the side of the cliff.

Had Tobin seen this place? It was not marked on his map, and Philip had not seen it during his previous attempts at reconnoitring.

Stupidly, he had not brought a light, but it would be risky to shine one about with the boat coming in, in any case. Hopefully, in the dinghy, Captain Frome was aware of the visitors, for Philip would not be able to reach the landing point in time. He felt around the cave as best he could, but hampered by the darkness, began to think he might be better served to come again early in the morning. As he turned to go, he heard a buzzing sound coming towards him, and he ducked just in time to miss a colony of bats take flight over his head. Rattled enough for the night, he abandoned the cave and headed back up the cliff to his room.

~

THE NEXT MORNING, Amelia awoke early, excited at the prospect of spending the day painting. When she made her way downstairs, a basket of food had been prepared for her, and a maid informed her that an easel and paints had been carried down to the beach. Amelia did not wait for Captain Elliot. Quite frankly, she needed some time to think. After repairing to her room to fetch a bonnet, she hurried out to the courtyard and down the steps to the beach with the basket of food her aunt had so thoughtfully had prepared for her.

Once standing before the easel, she studied her subject and wondered what, precisely, Captain Elliot wanted from her.

It was a fascinating place. The house stood atop the cliff and was only a small part of the whole. Amelia would never have guessed there were prisons and tunnels beneath had Captain Elliot not told her. Suddenly the mood to paint took hold, and she simply began to depict what she thought was best. Choosing an angle with the sun behind her, highlighting the ocean, the cliffs and the house on top, she loaded a brush to apply a wash of colour.

When she at length stood back to survey her work, a clapping sound nearly startled her out of her wits. She turned about.

"You nearly frightened me to death!"

"I have been here an hour and you did not even notice. Very impressive," Captain Elliot said, doubtless mocking her.

"I fear I become absorbed in my work, sir. I beg your pardon."

"Thankfully, no one was here to harm you. May I say it is probably not the best idea to lose yourself in the moment when working on an assignment?"

Amelia felt her cheeks flush. It was one thing she hated about her fair skin—she could never hide her embarrassment.

"It is of little consequence, now." He looked toward her painting. "Is this one for your aunt or for me?"

"I do not know. I was not certain what scene you might care for, so I simply painted."

He turned back to the cliffs. "Come here a moment. I want to show you something."

She did as he asked, and then he moved close behind her, disturbing her recently found peace. Once behind her, he rested his arm on her shoulder and pointed.

"Do you see the window, just below the chimney, on the north side?"

"Yes," she answered.

"That is my bedchamber. Just below that window, and across by about thirty feet, is a small cave."

"Oh, yes I see it! What is inside?"

"I do not know, yet. It was too dark last night to see."

"You climbed down to that cave? Are you insane?"

"Most likely," he replied amiably. "I suspect there are more of those, and that is what I would like you to look for as you paint."

"In a map form?"

"No, I think it is best if you keep to painting what you see. Tobin was gracious enough to visit me last night and draw a map. He was a prisoner here, you know."

"I had forgotten," she said quietly, not wanting to think of her aunt being a political pawn for Napoleon.

"Last night, the rascal decided to provide her guards below with a keg of brandy, and took the opportunity to explore a little further."

Amelia waited for him to elaborate, but he remained silent. "Are you going to tell me what he found?"

"Are you certain you wish to hear?"

"When you put it like that, of course I want to hear! If you only intend to infuriate me, you may leave me now."

"And forgo the delicious picnic your aunt provided? I think not. Come, be seated and I shall tell you what I found while we eat."

Amelia felt a sinking feeling inside, but it had been several hours since she had left the house, so she sat in one of the two wooden chairs left by the servants and accepted a piece of cheese, some fruit and a glass of apple cider from the Captain.

She took a few bites of food in between sips of her drink and soon felt much refreshed.

"Will you tell me what Tobin found?" she prompted when she felt prepared to hear it.

"First, there is some good news. He did not find any prisoners. He found only the guards."

"That is in agreement with what she told us."

"Indeed. The bad news, however, is that he found enough supplies to outfit an army for a lengthy war."

"What kind of supplies do you mean, exactly?" Amelia asked warily.

"Guns, swords, cannon, ammunition, fresh uniforms..."

"Enough!" She held up her hands. Her aunt had still not lied to her in so many words. "No olives?" she asked, attempting to lighten her mood.

"I asked the same question. Tobin did not notice any food stores other than brandy."

"Of course," she retorted. "What happens next?"

"I sent Tobin to report directly to Wellington. I suspect he will need to warn the King."

"King Louis?"

"Yes, a large proportion of his subjects are not loyal; it is too soon after the revolution. Whatever else he may or may not be, Napoleon is a leader of the people, I will allow him that."

"The situation is very similar to what happened in the colonies."

"True. I cannot fault any man for wishing for a better life. I must argue the difference, however. The people in the colonies tried to leave peacefully. They did not behead their leaders."

"Is that where you were going when the ship was wrecked?"

"Yes... to a war I was not certain I fully supported." He rubbed his chin. "But I should be careful what I say."

"Your words are safe with me. I know very little about the matter, but it seems the people were being taxed to an unfair degree."

"That was their claim, yes."

She wrinkled her nose. "I am very glad you are here, then. That is something I have never liked about war."

"Which part?" he asked with a chuckle.

"The part where soldiers are merely pawns of the rich, who sit in their comfortable castles and mansions, making decisions and playing chess with the lives of others. I doubt not most ordinary soldiers have no notion of what they are fighting for."

"At times, it does feel that way, but it has been the same since the dawn of time. A soldier always knows they are fighting for their country, though, and being under another country's rule is worse."

"I had not considered that. Mayhap you are right."

As they sat in peaceful contemplation, Amelia lifted her face to the sun.

"You are begging for more spots," Captain Elliot teased.

"At the moment I do not care. It feels glorious." She stole a sideways glance at him, and he was smiling at her. Their eyes met for a moment and her heart gave a little leap; immediately, she turned away. "When do you plan to explore the cave?" she asked, in an attempt to diffuse the awkwardness she felt.

"I should have done so at first light this morning, but I overslept," he admitted.

"What do you think is in there?"

"Perhaps nothing, but I must look."

"It seems as though it would be difficult to reach."

"It is. It would not be useful unless accessible from the inside."

"May I go with you?" she asked diffidently, keeping her gaze lowered as she played with a handful of sand, enjoying the cool feel of it running through her fingers.

"Absolutely not. It is extremely dangerous."

She huffed with irritation even though she had expected such a response. "May I at least keep a lookout for you?"

"I want you to stay in your bed, all nice and snug, and out of harm's way."

"And if you fall down the cliff?"

"I shall be dead, whether you are there or not."

"Why do you not use a rope?"

"I believe I shall," he answered smugly.

"Why will you not accept help? We are supposed to be partners."

"I am accepting your help. You are painting a map of sorts for me, and you are relating information to me. Speaking of which, I should probably escort you back to your aunt. The shadows are lengthening."

"Very well, if you insist on being stubborn."

"I do."

Amelia knew he was trying to protect her, but his rejection hurt her feelings nevertheless. She wanted to be part of the excitement, too.

"I think I know where it leads to," Captain Elliot remarked as she was packing up her paints.

Amelia looked up to the cave mouth to see her aunt standing nearby with a man Amelia could not make out from this distance.

"Do you think it leads to her private apartment?" she asked.

"I could not say, but it is my belief there is a vast area under the house which we have not yet found. Allow me," he said, taking the picnic basket. "We will return to the house before we are seen watching them."

CHAPTER 12

*P*hilip pulled himself out of bed just as the sun was creeping over the horizon. He knew it would be his best chance to look for whatever was in that hidden cave. Seeing La Glacier standing there yesterday had only confirmed it was some kind of secret entrance. He put on a jacket and trousers of bleached nankeen cloth, being close to the colour of the rocks should he be seen by any of the guards. Then he secured a rope he'd borrowed from the stables around the heaviest piece of furniture he could find— a solid walnut chest of drawers—so that he would have a safer and quicker way to return to his room.

He pushed into his pockets everything he could think he might need—a gun, a small lamp, and a drawing book and pencil. Checking the rope one more time, he had opened the window to climb out when he heard a light knock on his door.

Philip muttered a curse. He had locked it, of course, but now he had to answer.

For less than a second, he stared at Lady Amelia. Reaching out, he hauled her into his room and thrust the door to with a snap.

"What are you doing here?" he demanded in an angry whisper. "Do you realize you could compromise everything?"

"Good morning to you too, sir," she whispered. "I have come to make sure you are safe."

"You are more likely to cause the opposite," he snapped. This interference in his plans was not what he needed. Why had he trusted her with such information? "Very well. Since you are here, you can be my lookout. There is a spyglass on my table. Pull the rope three times if you see something I need to return for. Pull four times if there is danger and I need to remain below."

"Three to return, four to stay. I can manage that."

Philip climbed out of the window and hoped Amelia would do as she was told. With the aid of the rope, he scaled the cliff quickly. It was far less daunting by daylight. By his best estimate, it was only about thirty feet to the opening in the cliff and he tied the end of the rope around his waist once he reached the landing so he would feel Amelia's warnings should she need to give them.

It soon became dark inside, since the sun did not reach beyond the first few feet. He pulled out his lanthorn and lit it; before long he found a door, some fifteen feet or more hidden inside the cave. He tried the latch, and although it was rusted, it was not locked.

Once inside, he prayed he would not find any unpleasant surprises... such as a guard dog or bats...

It took a moment for his eyes to adjust to the light. The smell was much the same as the one he had noticed when below in Madame's office; a salty, musty odour of damp. Somewhere in the distance, there was the sound of dripping water, which indicated he was in a large, open space. He held up the lanthorn and was shocked to see how far the light spread in the vast cave. In fact, having walked as far as the rope could reach, he had to take it off in order to keep going.

It was similar to one of Wellington's war rooms. There were charts and maps covering the wall, and there was a large table filling the centre. Never would he have guessed this room existed had the Irish rogue not paid him a visit night before last! It was so well hidden away from the caves and tunnels near the beach.

"Aha!" he whispered when he came upon a model of an island. There were detailed plans of how they intended to remove the

Emperor, but he could not find a date. Philip began sorting through a pile of papers, trying desperately to find any sign of when it would happen. If La Glacier truly intended to leave when her nieces left, he and his comrades were going to be short of time to prepare. Over half the British army was fighting in America! How would they defend themselves?

"It has to be here somewhere!"

"What has to be here?" His heart all but stopped. Slowly looking up as he fought his sudden alarm, he saw Lady Amelia standing before him. She had managed to sneak up on him admirably. He was definitely losing his touch!

"What the devil are you doing in here?" He struggled to keep his voice to a whisper. Although his anger had to be evident, he was barely containing it.

"I was growing worried. You have been down here a very long time and I felt the tension on the rope give way."

"Did you scale the cliff?" he asked in disbelief, eyeing her skirts.

"I had practice once before climbing down a rope, if you recall when Thurgood kidnapped me."

Philip blew out a frustrated breath. "You are here now, so help me look."

"What are we looking for?"

"A date. I know what is planned, but I need to know when they mean to do it."

He continued searching through the stack of papers on the table while Amelia went over to the wall to look at the drawings there. Philip knew he had already been in the cave for nearly half an hour, and he needed to get out. He hated being so close and yet not have found the final piece of information he needed.

"We must go. We have been here too long." He swiftly made certain everything was back as he had found it. They had just turned to leave when they heard a lock rattle in the door at the end of the cavern.

"Quick! Under the table!" Grabbing her arm, he pulled her down with him, making certain he was protecting her before turning out the light.

She was doing an excellent job of remaining still. Despite his years of practice, he still heard the blood pounding wildly through his ears whenever he was in danger of being caught.

The door swung open slowly, creaking on its hinges. A few small steps sounded on the stone floor, and light spread around the room.

"I must be hearing things," a female voice said faintly as small feet walked directly in front of their hiding place. Amelia tensed and he increased his grip on her as a warning. Philip heard footsteps move away again, evidently returning to the door, for it creaked as it was closed, followed by the jingle of keys locking it back in place. Strange is was locked from that side, but where did it lead that direction?

Amelia let out the breath she had obviously been holding and relaxed in his arms.

"We need to get out of here at once, before she alerts her guards. Follow me."

Philip did not dare to turn his lamp up again. He put an arm about Lady Amelia's body in silent command and they crawled back to where he had loosened the rope. Having helped Lady Amelia to her feet, he tied the rope around her waist and they hurried back to the cave opening.

"I will follow you," he directed, and once she had found her second foothold, he duly began to climb behind her.

They climbed in silence for perhaps three or four minutes, until Lady Amelia lost her footing and sent a spray of stones and grit into his face. 'Twas no more than he deserved for enjoying her ankles as she climbed.

"It seems far harder going up," she remarked as he let out a low curse.

"It is easy to think too much when you have just been nearly caught. Take a deep breath and take your time."

"Of course," she muttered. He saw her inhale and then she continued to climb the cliff admirably, despite her long skirts. She needed his assistance to crest the windowsill, but to his enormous relief they achieved their return without apparent detection. They both fell onto the floor, breathing heavily, and exchanged exhausted smiles.

"We won through," she said, her voice breathy and seductive in a way he was sure she was unaware.

"I should throttle you," he chided, still angry that she had disobeyed his orders. However, she looked so beautiful sitting there on his bedchamber floor, her hair dishevelled and her cheeks a rosy hue, that he was sorely tempted to break the rules.

"You cannot punish me for being concerned about you."

"I certainly can if it means you directly disobeyed orders."

"Very well," she conceded and folded her arms over her chest, which, he could not help but note, was still heaving.

It was the same feeling no matter whether it came post-battle or post-chase. There was some kind of devil's brew running through your veins which made you want to do things you would otherwise know better than to even consider. Leaning forward, he kissed her the way he had wanted to the other day. The feel of her sweet mouth beneath his was a fuse to his disordered senses and thoughts of gentleness were forgotten. He kissed her with a primal tension he had been holding inside for days. Cradling her head to his, he angled his mouth over hers and kissed her hard. The resistance he had been expecting was not there as she fully joined in the exchange of passion from the beginning. What she lacked in experience, she made up for with zeal, which was not at all helpful in reminding him to stop. It was only when her hand strayed to his neckcloth that he was able to think coherently enough to pull back.

"Forgive me. I should know better," he said, running his hand through his hair.

"Forgive yourself. I, for one, feel much better now."

"I beg your pardon?" he asked as she rose to her feet.

"At first, I was feeling strange, as though something inside me was about to explode. Since you... kissed me... I feel quite normal again." She smoothed down her skirts and walked calmly to the door, where she cast him one almost apologetic smile before looking to see if the hallway was clear and then slipping away.

He continued to stare at the door long after she had left. He did not think he would ever feel normal again.

AMELIA HOPED she had appeared indifferent as she left Captain Elliot's room. She had completely forgotten where she was and what she was doing. Once she had gathered her wandering wits, she had had to leave before she became a drivelling fool. Her legs had felt like jelly as she tottered to her bedchamber, and in colour, her cheeks must have been the brightest shade of red. They still burned as though she had been seated too close to a roaring fire. She would never be remotely close to normal again. No doubt Captain Elliot experienced kisses like that often, and she did not want him to know how much it had affected her.

A knock sounded on the door and Amelia jumped. "Silly girl!" she muttered under her breath. "Enter."

"Good morning, sister," Meg said in greeting as she came in and closed the door behind her. She looked pale and somewhat ill, and put a hand to her mouth when she sat down in a chair by the window.

"How are you feeling?" Amelia asked.

"It would be better if I knew where you were this morning."

Amelia debated telling an untruth, but this was her sister.

"Luke saw you creep out of your bedchamber when he was going to fetch me some ginger tea—it was early and we did not wish to disturb the servants. He saw you enter Captain Elliot's room."

Amelia swallowed hard. She thought she had been so careful! "It is true. However, it is not what you think."

Meg raised a single brow and narrowed her gaze at her.

"We were exploring a cave in the side of a cliff. I swear it!"

"Then why do you look so guilty and your lips so swollen? I think you have been thoroughly kissed, Amelia! Luke will be speaking to Captain Elliot about this," she said fiercely.

"No!" Amelia objected. "Please assure him nothing untoward has happened. I do not need any interference from Luke. It was nothing."

Meg sighed and leaned back into the chair in a slouch at variance with her usual correct posture.

"I do not like this affair one little bit, Amelia. I do not know why I agreed to this charade."

"It is all rather peculiar," Amelia agreed.

"Well, we are here for the nonce and must make the best of it. We must complete our business, the sooner to return home."

Amelia felt a strange sensation inside at the thought of returning to England. For some reason, she was not certain it sat well with her.

"Oh, by the by," Meg said as she stood to go. "Wellington is coming for a visit. He is expected this afternoon. Do you know what that is about?"

"I could not venture to say," Amelia answered. She did not think Tobin could have reached his Grace yet; perhaps they had missed each other along the way.

"I suppose it will enliven things rather. Luke is concerned it will stir up more danger. Shall I see you at breakfast?"

"Yes. I will be down directly."

Meg leaned over and kissed her on the forehead. "Please be careful, Amelia. I do not wish to see you hurt." She turned and left the room, closing the door softly behind her.

"I fear it is too late for that," Amelia whispered. Thoughtfully, she touched the tips of her fingers to her lips and turned to look at herself in the glass.

"What am I doing?" She would have to face Captain Elliot over and over again, and she did not know if she could do it with equanimity. With a sigh, she closed her eyes and tried to steel herself for his indifference when they met again. If she could not show herself to be unperturbed about it, everyone would see through her dissimulation.

She rang for her maid and while she waited, held a damp cloth from the wash-basin over her lips.

Her maid helped her to dress in a simple white frock, despite her aunt's predilection for the colour, and styled her hair simply, for she was feeling very subdued.

"What has you in the doldrums, milady?" her maid asked with concern.

"Nothing of any moment, Alice. I will be quite myself after a cup of coffee," she replied in an attempt to tease.

"I am right sorry, my lady. I should have brought you a cup. I will fetch one at once," the woman said, fretting at her lapse.

"No, no. I am not upset with you. I am on my way to breakfast now."

The maid bobbed a curtsy and went about her other tasks.

Amelia went down to the breakfast parlour and was relieved when Captain Elliot was absent. The remainder of the party was there, however, and the gentlemen stood when she entered.

After she was seated, a footman placed a cup of coffee before her and for some minutes she concentrated on its healing powers while the conversation continued around her.

"Since we will be having more company, I have decided we should plan some entertainment. Amelia, do you have any suggestions for amusement?" her aunt asked.

"Wellington enjoys dancing," she proposed.

"He also enjoys a good hunt," Waverley added.

"*Oui*, someone mentioned his prime hunter is in the stable."

"I doubt very much that he expects grand entertainment, Madame," Meg added. "Perhaps he only wishes for a reprieve from Paris and good company."

"Of course. What else could he hope to find here? Where is our good captain this morning?"

"I am here, Madame," that gentleman answered as he walked into the room and bent over her hand. "I beg your pardon, I overslept... perhaps as a result of too much of your fine brandy."

"You may do as you please here, Captain Elliot. We were just discussing the impending arrival of your commander."

"Wellington? He is coming here?" Captain Elliot looked astonished.

"It surprises you as well," she remarked.

"I am no longer his troop, if you recall, Madame. I am no longer privy to his movements. He is jolly good company, though."

"We thought to arrange an evening of dancing, and perhaps some hunting."

"Combined with your excellent food and drink, that will be more than sufficient to please him," Captain Elliot reassured her.

"I am glad to hear it. Nieces, I thought to go into the village today, if you would care to accompany me? It is quaint and charming, and also happens to boast a fine collection of silks."

"That sounds delightful," Meg said, while Amelia smiled.

"Excellent, I will be waiting with the carriage at noon, *non?*"

Her aunt seemed to have lost some of her composure. What could that be about? Did the thought of Wellington visiting scare her?

Lisette hurried from the room. Had anyone else noticed the change? Amelia's eye caught Captain Elliot's and the look on his face confirmed she had not imagined it.

"Excuse me." Amelia set down her cup and hastened after her aunt.

She had moved quickly, Amelia thought as she followed. When she reached her aunt's apartments, the door was already shut. Amelia knocked softly but did not hear an answer. Perhaps her aunt had gone elsewhere. Putting her ear to the door and listening carefully, she heard the unmistakeable sound of muffled sobbing. Turning the handle quietly, she peeped into the room. Her normally imperturbable aunt was sitting on a bench next to her bed; she had her head in her hands and she was crying. Amelia ran over at once and put her arms around her.

It only caused her to sob harder.

Amelia remembered her mother doing this very thing. She would hold her tightly until the tears had run dry, and say the best medicine was having a good cry. Amelia therefore sat and held her aunt until she composed herself.

"Oh, dear. I had not intended for you to see me in such straits," she said, sitting up and dabbing at her eyes with a handkerchief.

"Mama used to hold me like that when I needed to cry."

Her aunt smiled weakly. "She used to do the same for me."

"Is there something you wish to talk about?" Amelia asked gently.

"*Non.* It is silly, really. My emotions are simply shaken."

"Is this our fault?" Amelia asked. "We can leave you. Or is it because the Duke of Wellington is coming?"

"*Non, non!*" She shook her head violently. "Wellington and I are old acquaintances, despite our differing loyalties, and your presence has been a gift I will cherish. This has nothing to do with you. Lannes and I had a disagreement."

"Perhaps when his temper cools he will be more reasonable."

Her aunt raised her hand and caressed the side of Amelia's face lovingly. "If it were only that simple, my dear. Things will work out as they should. Now, enough of my troubles. What of your beau? I fear I have neglected you dreadfully, and I only hope to make up for it."

"Captain Elliot has been all that is attentive," Amelia reassured her.

"Perhaps Wellington's visit will have at least one good outcome," she said. "We will be unable to hide away in our chambers any longer."

"That is very true. I will leave you to your solace, Aunt. I apologize for intruding but I am not sorry if I gave you a measure of comfort."

"You did, *mon cher.*"

Amelia wandered back to her apartments, trying desperately to reconcile this aunt with the one who organized armies and plotted wars. Was it possible for such disparity in the same person?

CHAPTER 13

While the ladies went on an excursion to the village, Philip set out to greet Wellington before he entered the fortress. He rode alongside the ladies' equipage as far as the village and excused himself on the pretence of surveying the area. There was no telling when Wellington would arrive, but Philip stopped at the fork in the road and dismounted by the stream where he had met Tobin only a couple of weeks ago. How long ago that seemed.

Fortunately, he did not have much above an hour to wait. As he saw the group of horses and riders approaching, he recognized Old Hookey's hat and distinctive chestnut horse, and he stepped out into the road to intercept them.

There were a few people accompanying the Duke, as would be expected, but Tobin was also among the entourage, which took Philip by surprise.

"Your Grace," Philip said in greeting. "May I speak with you before you proceed?" He turned to Tobin. "Lieutenant O'Neill, you made excellent time if you have already been to Paris and back."

"We were fortunate enough to meet along the way." interposed Wellington, swinging himself to the ground and handing his reins to an aide. "I was travelling to Calais when I decided to detour here, based on the news we had received. Have you discovered anything else in O'Neill's absence?"

"Indeed, we have, sir. Lady Amelia and I found a hidden cave which is being used as a war room."

"Excellent work, Elliot," Wellington said approvingly. They walked a few feet away from the escort, which followed the Field Marshal's gestured command by also dismounting to stretch their legs and rest their horses.

"Everything was detailed, sir—maps, routes, ships, stores needed—everything except for the date they intend to strike. However, I expect they plan to act quickly, since it appears she is making preparations for a journey."

"If she does intend to leave soon and return immediately to France, that only leaves us a few weeks to prepare. I intend to pass the information onto the Foreign Office immediately. It is a dashed nuisance that so many of our good men are in America. This is not going to go down well with Parliament. It will take some persuading to get the help we need."

"It does not bode well, that is for certain. They are prepared and plan to take us off our guard."

"Yes, we must come up with a way to stop them, Elliot."

"How long do you intend to stay here, if I may be so bold?"

"Only one night, now. I must deliver this news myself. First, we must discover what we can and then we need to get word to King Louis and our allies."

"What else would you like me to do, sir?" Philip asked.

Wellington stroked Copenhagen's nose as he thought. "How much do you think La Glacier suspects?"

"Most of it, I am afraid. She has been toying with us from the start."

"She is confident enough in her plans, then, that she does not fear our retribution. It has ever been the same with Napoleon...and now her."

"I do not believe she knows we have discovered her secret room."

"You have found out what we had need of for the present. We

should anticipate an imminent attempt to help Napoleon escape. There is little we can do about it. Many on the island are loyal to him and will look the other way. Hopefully the navy will deal with him, but we must be prepared, come what may. I may try to talk some sense into Madame."

"You do not think her too far committed to the cause?" Philip asked with astonishment.

"It never hurts to try."

They remounted their horses and Philip led the company to the gate of the fortress. The ladies were returning in the carriage at the same time, and they waved before guiding Wellington's party up the path to the house.

"Welcome to my home, *Monsieur le Duc*," La Glacier said in greeting. She had adopted her cold demeanour once again. Was it unhappiness, or was there something else on her mind when she was hosting the enemy?

Philip observed her interchanges with Wellington very closely. She still seemed disturbed but was clearly trying hard to remain aloof.

He was as charming as ever and bowed over her hand. "I must express my gratitude for your hospitality. I regret I can only stay one night before returning to England."

"That is a pity, indeed," La Glacier replied with no emotion. "I consider it a great honour that you have condescended to visit my château."

"The honour is entirely mine."

Indicating with her hand for him to follow, she turned and began making her way into the house. Several servants in smart livery were lined up to welcome the famous Duke, and beneath his hat, Philip caught Josefina's eye. He affected no notice of her and hoped Tobin would distract her, although there really was not much harm she could do if she recognized him. It would be her word against his, in any case. Philip looked around but Tobin was nowhere in sight.

"I will have tea served soon in the drawing room if you would care to refresh yourself first, your Grace. My housekeeper will show you to your apartments," La Glacier said to Wellington as they walked into the marble entrance hall.

Philip took off his hat and coat, and draping it over his arm, began to climb the stairs.

"Psst. Psst." He heard a hissing sound from an alcove. He was afraid to look and kept walking.

"*Monsieur!*" an urgent female voice whispered.

He could not avoid the confrontation when she stepped directly in front of him.

"May I help you, *mademoiselle?*" he asked in a haughty, aristocratic voice, feigning complete ignorance.

"Do not pretend you do not know me," she said, hurt in her large, brown eyes.

"I am afraid you are mistaken."

"There cannot be two of you. I know it." She put her hands on her hips, expressing in the age-old gesture the wrath of a woman betrayed.

Footsteps sounded in the corridor and her face assumed a look of fear. "I will come to you later. We are not finished."

"I think we are, *mademoiselle,*" he said curtly.

"There you are!" Lady Amelia said as she rounded the corner.

"Did you have a nice trip to the village, my love?" he asked as the maid Josefina turned her back to them and pretended to be cleaning a statue in the alcove.

He linked his arm through Amelia's and drew her away, whispering in her ear, "Say nothing. The maid was trying to arrange an assignation."

"How dare she!" Amelia looked back, a glare marring her beautiful countenance. Josefina made no secret of glaring back. "I will speak to my aunt about her!"

He pulled her along the gallery with him. "You will do no such thing. She was my informant and recognized me."

"She looks more like a woman scorned," Amelia remarked astutely.

Philip gave a small shrug.

"You horrible man!" she said, hitting him on the arm. He led her to her apartments. There was little he could say in his defence. It was part of the job.

"I will see you directly." With an unladylike glower, Amelia shut the door in his face, but then opened it again. "Wait," she started to call, but he was still standing there, feeling vastly amused.

"Yes?"

"You are odious," she fumed.

"Is that all you wish to say? How disappointing."

"No, but...something is amiss with my aunt," she whispered.

"What do you mean?" Philip frowned and leaned forward. He could see her hesitate. "Amelia, you must tell me."

"She had an argument with Lannes. I found her crying about it."

"When was this?" he demanded.

"This morning, when I followed her from the breakfast room."

"Ah, yes. I thought you were indisposed," he said with a wry grin.

She looked exasperated. "I have not seen the man since last evening. Have you?"

"Come to think of it, no."

"It must have been serious. It takes a great deal to shake her composure."

"Perhaps they argued over Wellington's visit. Lannes could not be pleased about it."

"She was given little choice," Amelia added.

"I believe his visit is having the effect he wanted."

"Yes, he seems to be stirring the pot nicely. I just do not wish to see my aunt hurt. Now you may leave. I am still not pleased with you." She shut the door firmly in his face again.

AMELIA KNEW Captain Elliot was a rogue, but somehow she had hoped he was different. The look on that maid's face had been murderous.

As she dressed for dinner, she wondered what was left for Meg and herself to do. She and Captain Elliot had confirmed plans to free

Napoleon and evidence of a rebel army. Was anything else required of her? What would Wellington do with the knowledge?

That was something she must know. It was one thing to discover information against her aunt, and another thing entirely to aid in harming her physically.

For the coming evening, Amelia donned a black silk gown of slender design which was elegant without excess adornment other than an overdress of black lace. This added texture but no frills. The gown had a low neck and small, capped sleeves that hung over her shoulders. A double string of pearls wound around her neck, and a few curls of her dark red locks fell over her shoulders. Although she was both angry and hurt, she felt a new sense of confidence in herself. As the assignment was drawing to a close, she realized she had been equal to the task and somehow that made her feel as if she could face England again, alone.

She pulled her black silk gloves up above her elbow and place a bracelet of pearls over each. After dabbing her favourite scent of violets on each side of her neck, she left to join the others downstairs.

The party was gathered in the drawing room, and Amelia noted Lannes' continued absence. Meg was standing next to their aunt; together they were a vision of beauty, their aunt in her customary white, and Meg, dressed in pale pink, resembling a fair English rose.

Wellington, Waverley, and Elliot were helping themselves to the fine brandy, set ready on a silver tray. Standing all together, they presented a strikingly handsome picture of manhood.

Captain Elliot looked up at her entrance and his gaze arrested. Her heart twisted. It was a bitter-sweet pleasure to know that she had had some effect on him. It was not practised or false, but it did mean nothing more than attraction existed between them.

Amelia crushed the inner sadness she felt and tried instead to project the confidence she had gained despite her hurt. Knowing they might be at odds over how to deal with her aunt—not to mention the matter of the maid—Amelia tried to distance her feelings for the Captain.

"Ah, niece, what a striking picture you present." Aunt Lisette cast her gaze over Captain Elliot. "We are complete now. An intimate party we make, do we not, just the six of us?"

Dinner was announced and she was left to be escorted by the Captain.

"You look beautiful," he said softly as they walked behind the other couples.

"Thank you," she murmured. She could not bring herself to meet his eyes. It would be easier to separate herself from him that way. The more distance, the better. She resolutely ignored the sinking feeling in her chest.

After they were seated and a tomato bisque was served, Amelia could feel someone's perusal. She glanced around the room from under her lashes as she sipped her soup. Whoever the person was, they were not Captain Elliot or anyone else at the table. How strange, she mused. Could she be imagining it?

Dismissing her concerns, she continued to sip her bisque. The feeling, however, would not go away.

As the servants removed the soup, and placed the next dish in front of them, she saw who had been staring... the maid from earlier. She met the girl's eye and the murderous glare she had imagined was still present. Amelia shivered. Did this maid think her a threat? She glanced at Captain Elliot but he did not appear to have noticed. Either that, or he was ignoring her, which was a very lowering thought.

Perhaps servants in France thought they were entitled to dally—or more—with the members of the household and their guests, and maybe Amelia needed to disabuse the wench of her misapprehension. So lost in contemplation of how to confront this brazen servant was she, Amelia barely tasted her food during the remainder of the meal.

"Amelia, are you feeling quite the thing?" Meg asked.

"Oh, I beg your pardon. I was wool-gathering."

"Not in France, I gather," she retorted.

"Where is your man, Madame?" Wellington asked Aunt Lisette. "I thought he left your side only to sleep."

"He left," Aunt Lisette replied succinctly.

"Well, that is good news for me," he replied jovially. "I can dance with you all night."

"You really do love to dance," she remarked.

"Only when there are beautiful partners," he replied in a reflective tone.

"Very well, we can arrange a little dancing after dinner." Aunt Lisette nodded to a servant, who scurried away.

They finished their meal without any further awkwardness, and Amelia was glad to escape the hateful eyes of the maid.

She was, of course, partnered with Captain Elliot for the first dance, and she was glad for the opportunity to unleash her fears.

Captain Elliot took her hand in his and put his other hand on her waist. While she had anticipated this from the music, the sensation of a gentleman's hand on her person always sent a shock through her. It was commonplace to waltz in France, and Amelia did enjoy it so. The restrictions upon it in England only made it possible to perform it at large balls in London.

"Is something wrong?" Captain Elliot asked. "You seemed to be in a world of your own during dinner."

"That is because I was," she retorted. "*Your* maid was shooting daggers at me for the entire meal!"

"Ah, the maid. I should have guessed as much. She was also staring at me a goodly part of the time."

"It is a wonder she was able to perform her duties. What did you do to her?"

"Why must everyone assume the worst? I did nothing more than carry on a flirtation with her in order to try to obtain information. She was not even very useful in that endeavour," he complained.

"Nothing occurred between you at all?" Amelia looked at him sceptically. "For someone who received naught more than words, she is quite possessive of you."

He had the grace to look guilty.

"What did you do?" She narrowed her gaze at him—she could hardly do anything more while dancing.

He turned her and dipped her rakishly backwards, clearly trying to avoid the question. It would not work.

"Tell me. I must know what I am dealing with," she insisted.

"I gave her one small kiss, that is all. I swear it!"

She would have let the matter drop, but he continued.

"Besides, Tobin is sweet on her. I was led to believe they were quite happy together."

She snorted, uncaring of rudeness she would usually abhor. "Obviously not."

"It would not be the first time he has stretched the truth," Philip observed.

"Speaking of Tobin, where is he?"

"Perhaps he did not wish to blow his cover as I did. I did not admit anything of the sort to the maid, but I could not convince her otherwise."

"Yes. If she felt doubly betrayed, imagine the wrath."

Philip laughed. "I do not imagine that my charms are enough to send any female into raptures let alone rage. Her feelings are only hurt because I did not pretend to know her."

"Do not forget you then called me 'my love.'" That would throw salt on any female's tender sensibilities."

"I am not as callous as that. I did not mean it that way. I thought she would realize I was not *Monsieur Lefebre* if she thought you were my love."

"At any rate, I hope we do not have to see her again. I assume our stay will not be for much longer since we have the information we sought."

"I do not have direct orders on that front, yet," he said quietly, looking up, Amelia noticed, presumably to see where La Glacier was. Wellington had brought a smile to her aunt's lips, which was good.

"I presume to agree with you, however, we cannot directly stop your aunt from pursuing any of her actions. She is a free woman in a free country, despite her allegiance to the Emperor."

"As long as she does not admit such a thing publicly," Amelia pointed out.

Captain Elliot inclined his head as the waltz drew to a close.

Partners were exchanged for two more dances, and then Meg withdrew, claiming fatigue.

Waverley and Meg said good night, and retired.

Wellington took out his pocket watch and grunted his disapproval. "Would you perhaps show me the view from the outdoors?" he requested. "I received a hint of it from my room, but nothing is quite the same as the wind blowing in your face and the briny smell of the sea."

"*Oui*, of course, your Grace. Perhaps you missed your calling for the navy," La Glacier said with a sly smile.

"And have missed the greatest rivalry of our time on land? I think not. Besides, you cannot have a proper ball or ride horses on a ship."

"No, indeed. Come, we shall take in the view from the courtyard."

Captain Elliot offered Amelia his arm and she placed her fingers on it. They followed behind Wellington and Aunt Lisette.

"Whatever was wrong earlier, he seems to have made her forget about it for the present," Captain Elliot observed.

"I am glad of it."

"What a beautiful night," Wellington's voice boomed ahead.

Without warning, a scream of terror rent the air. It had come from her aunt. Amelia and Captain Elliot hastened forward.

Wellington had his arms around Aunt Lisette and was trying to pull her away from whatever had elicited such a ghastly response from her. Amelia gasped in horror and pressed her hands to her mouth. Hanging from a tree at the edge of the courtyard was La Glacier's man, Lannes, quite dead.

Amelia could not restrain a shudder. Without a word, Wellington turned Aunt Lisette's sobbing face into his coat and led her back inside.

Amelia stared at the body. She had never seen a man hanged before, and she had not imagined anything so violent, even though she knew criminals were served that form of justice. The man's eyes stared blankly, his skin pallid, and his features were bloated.

"Why?" The single word was all that escaped her lips. Once

Captain Elliot had assured himself the man was indeed dead, he put his arm around her for comfort.

"It is a warning."

She could not but agree with him... yet who was being warned? Them or her aunt?

CHAPTER 14

*L*ady Amelia has gone upstairs to comfort her aunt," Wellington informed Waverley as they joined Philip in the study.

"A deuced bad business," Wellington said as he paced the length of the room. "And on my watch, no less. Very bad."

"Should we call the authorities?" Waverley asked.

"Madame Lisette asked me not to. She said she would take care of it in the morning after we have departed."

"We?" Philip questioned.

"Yes. She thinks it best if everyone leaves. She feels his death was precipitated by our presence, and I am inclined to agree. It is certainly an unfortunate coincidence."

"I agree it is best if we leave," Waverley said. "Meg has been uncomfortable with the whole business. You have found what you were looking for."

Philip disagreed. He did not think all the loose ends were yet quite tied up. "You are content to leave things as they are?" he asked Wellington.

"What else can I do?" Wellington asked in return, holding his hands wide apart. "This was an exercise in gathering information which I cannot act on. It is not a crime to gather supplies—or men. Until she does something illegal with them, our hands are tied."

"Does that include the information we found in the cave?"

"It does. You yourself admitted there was no indication of date or time associated with it. We can keep an eye on matters, but there is no point in putting the ladies in further danger here."

"I agree. We will plan on setting sail with you in the morning," Waverley said with finality. Wishing them good night again, he nodded a salute and left the room.

"Help me deal with the body," Wellington commanded. "It is the least we can do for Madame Lisette. She is quite shaken."

Philip followed his commander to the courtyard. He wondered whether La Glacier was shaken because she had ordered Lannes' execution or because she feared for her own safety. She had almost sentenced him to death along with Hawthorne, and it was nothing short of a miracle he was here today. Wordlessly, Philip held the dead body for Wellington while he cut it down from the tree and sliced away the ropes.

"She wants it taken down near the rocks on the beach," the Duke directed.

"To make it look like an accident," Philip muttered as they carried their heavy burden down a hundred or more steps. Philip could not help but recall being left to his fate on this very beach, next to this very rock behind which they placed Lannes.

"He will be gone by morning," Philip remarked.

"With any luck, and if God wills it so," Wellington agreed.

"Who do you think did this? Do you think it was her?"

Wellington shook his head. "Someone from the ranks who thinks she is going soft in her allegiance."

"Someone with an eye on taking her place?"

"Or the Emperor's."

"Do you think she has a chance of freeing him?"

"If anyone can, she can," Wellington said, staring at the vast ocean and stars which had now come out to greet them. "I do not wish to be caught off guard, Elliot."

"Nor I, sir."

"Signal Frome. I want to inform him of our change in plan and discover if he saw anything."

Philip took a flint and steel from his pocket and struck it, lighting the small taper he kept with it for such uses. He flashed it three times and watched for a response. After a couple of minutes, there was a reciprocal three flashes and they waited for the boat to draw near. It was a moonless night, and Philip could envisage the smugglers plying their trade with vigour all along the coasts between here and England.

As the boat drew closer, Philip flashed the light again to direct Frome towards the beach and away from the rocks.

Wellington stood there in silence. There had to be a great deal on his mind, with the knowledge they had obtained regarding La Glacier and Napoleon's intentions. Philip did not envy Old Hookey his task of trying to gain more support from Parliament when the Peninsular War had just ended and many regiments were already fighting another conflict on the shores of America.

The boat was coming in to shore, and the two of them stepped forward to guide it.

Captain Frome was standing at the hull, and Philip held out a hand for him to climb over the edge.

"Captain," Wellington said by way of greeting.

"Your Grace!"

"We have a change in plans. We are all departing on the morrow. I want to know if you have seen anything suspicious?"

"There was some activity in and out of the caves. The man who visited the first day returned, but I have witnessed nothing out of the ordinary. Has something occurred?" Frome asked.

"La Glacier's henchman was murdered today."

"Lannes?" Frome let out a low whistle.

"Quite," Wellington agreed. "It is not good for us to be here."

"Should we not dispose of the contraband we found?"

"No. We have no grounds to at this point, and would only anger La Glacier and, in his turn, Napoleon. Even if he does escape, we have no proof he will try to retake the throne...yet. I intend to leave men here on watch, and return to England to raise support for what I believe is to come."

"Shall I remain here to keep a lookout or return to England?" Frome asked.

"Return. I only wanted you here for extra protection with the ladies' presence."

"Yes, sir. I will be ready to depart at first light." Philip and Wellington watched Frome's craft pull away and mounted the steps back to the fortress. When they reached the courtyard, Wellington began to take his leave, but Philip could see he remembered something, for he turned and raised his finger.

"The Lieutenant."

"Do you wish me to inform him to be ready to depart?"

Wellington wrinkled his brow.

"I think he would not be opposed to remaining," Philip suggested.

"The wind blows that way, does it? Very well. He can remain. Be sure to be ready to leave after breakfast."

"Yes, sir."

After watching his commander climb the grand staircase, Philip set out to look for Tobin.

The house was surprisingly quiet for having just experienced a violent death. Perhaps the occupants were all terrified of the same fate and were hiding in their rooms.

He crept down the servants' stairs with the idea of leaving that way to find Tobin, the passage only lit by a few sparse candles. He was a guest, so he could come and go as he pleased, but with Josefina thinking she recognized him, he did not want to take his chances with the guards.

There was light coming from the kitchen, so not everyone was abed. He knew it was likely some of the servants would have their quarters nearby, and when he heard giggles coming from behind one of the doors, his suspicions were confirmed.

He spied the door to his freedom, and was moving quietly on tiptoe past the door from where the sounds were emanating, when he heard the all too familiar voice. Cursing under his breath, he stopped, debating what he should do. Should he wait there until Tobin left? It could be a while, and he had no intention of listening to giggles and flirtatious nonsense for hours.

Philip supposed he could go into the village and leave a note for the Irishman at his rooms, but that was a long way when the rogue was right here.

Heavy footsteps approached the kitchen, and Philip had to make a quick decision. Skimming the big open room with his eyes, he saw there were few hiding places available to him, so he chose a shelf under one of the tables, amongst some sundry cooking utensils, and tried to cover himself as best he could.

The loud steps entered the kitchen, echoing off the stone walls. From his low vantage point, Philip watched a pair of heavy, worn boots cross the flagged floor and stop in front of the door where Tobin, and presumably Josefina, were fraternizing.

A heavy fist pounded upon the door.

"Josie!" the voice demanded, "I know you are in there!"

Philip strained to see who was knocking.

Josefina's face peered around the door. "What are you doing here, Pierre?"

Pierre? Philip asked himself. Pierre was a common name, but Pierre was the man whom La Glacier had sent away from the cave and whom Frome had said he saw today. Was this another one of Josefina's lovers spurned? Philip was beginning to feel rather cheap.

"You should not be here, brother. Did not Madame tell you not to return?"

Brother. That gives some little comfort, he thought, knowing it was but a crumb.

"Are you not going to invite your brother in?" Pierre asked in an irritated tone.

"Now is not a good time," she answered, her own voice low. Philip could see she was holding the door fast against her body.

"Who is it this time?" Pierre asked. He smacked one fist into the other hand. Philip desperately wanted to see the man's face. His voice seemed eerily familiar.

"It is none of your business."

"Is it the pedlar? It had better not be one of those Englishmen! I heard they are all leaving soon. Good riddance," he spat.

"How would you know?" she scolded. "Madame does not tell you anything anymore."

"That is about to change, you wait and see."

"What are you planning, Pierre? Tell me!"

"Nothing to worry your pretty little head over, but there are about to be some big changes coming."

"You had better be careful," she whispered. The words vibrated with warning.

"Lannes is no longer here to stand in my way," he boasted.

"What did you do, brother?" she asked, her horror clear.

"What should have been done a long time ago." The man finally took a couple of steps back and turned around so Philip could see his face. It was the man Philip had tied up on the road, the day he and Amelia had left Paris.

"Humph," Josefina responded.

"Soon you will have your rightful place here," he said, trying to tempt her with Spanish coin.

"I would be happy enough with a small cottage. It is when the guests come here, acting all high and mighty, I cannot abide it. There's a lady here who is Madame's niece. Flaunting herself at me. I'd like to see her taken down a notch or two."

"One of the English?" he asked.

"She has hair like fire. You cannot miss her."

"If you anger Madame..."

"What will she do? She should thank me for doing her a service. They've been spying on her, plain as day, and she does nothing!"

"Spying, eh? Maybe we can use this to our advantage," he said, scratching his beard in contemplation.

"We can talk tomorrow," Josefina said. "Now, leave me be." She kissed him on the cheek and shut the door in his face.

Philip sighed and resigned himself to a long wait under the table until Tobin emerged.

～

AMELIA LEFT her aunt in the hands of her maid, who had just adminis-tered a sleeping draught. Aunt Lisette had been inconsolable, and she appeared to be a woman in the depths of despair. She had said very little while Amelia had held her, except to insist that Amelia leave France at once, for her own safety. It had been difficult for her aunt to utter those words, Amelia could tell, and her heart ached. It felt as though she were torn between two worlds and one was forbidden to the other. Why did it have to be that way? Why must she be forced to choose?

Wiping a tear away, she walked down the hall, lost in the torment of her thoughts and feelings. When she reached her chamber, the painting she had begun of the fortress sat on an easel waiting for the finishing touches. For a few moments she studied its composition, the blue sky and the warm sunlight that bathed the stone château sitting atop the majestic cliffs overlooking the open water. She wanted to present it to her aunt as a gift. Since it was unlikely she would find rest in her bed that night, Amelia set about the task of completing the work.

Moving the easel in front of the lamp, she opened the windows to the cold night. Even though she could not see, the breeze and smell of the ocean transported her back to the morning on the beach, when she had felt free. Something had changed in her since then. Although she could not say what it was, she knew nothing would be the same after becoming close to her aunt, becoming close to Captain Elliot, and seeing that poor man hanging in the courtyard.

Amelia swallowed hard, trying to push the visions of the man from her mind, and then went about the task of finishing her work. A tear fell as she painted small touches on the beach, making her recall the picnic she had shared with Captain Elliot: the crab playing hide-and-seek with them, the shells she had found scattered across the sand, and the waves as they crawled forward then retreated, murmuring a gentle lullaby. She paused to listen to nature's song again and could almost feel the spray of the salty water on her face.

She smiled and inhaled deeply of the cool air, becoming lost in the memory.

A gentle sigh escaped her lips; at the same instant, a heavy object struck her on the head.

When next she opened her eyes, Amelia was completely disoriented. She was lying on a hard floor; it was dark, cold and damp, and she was bound hand and foot.

What had happened? Where was she? Closing her eyes, she tried to still her tumultuous thoughts to consider her predicament, but the back of her head hurt terribly and was pounding fit to burst. Her fingers were numb with cold, the tight bindings chafed her wrists and ankles, and her body was sore from lying on the rough stone. She began to shake with fear. There was a foetid stench reminiscent of the woods in winter, combined with that of rotten fish. Where was she? Who could have done this to her? Would she be left alone here to die? How long had she been gone? Would anyone have missed her yet? When the questions ran dry, she again tried to gather her wits. Had she not been warned to be alert at all times? She had felt safe in her room and had let her guard down. What a wretched spy she was!

She struggled against the bonds around her hands and ankles. They seemed to be fabric and she thought she might have a chance of loosening them if she worked at them enough. In spite of the cold, beads of perspiration formed on her brow with the effort. After several minutes of striving to be free, her hands also became numb and she had to stop.

It was difficult not to panic in the darkness. To keep from thinking about what might happen if no one found her, she surveyed what she could of her surroundings. The cold and damp indicated that, in all likelihood, she had been taken down into the maze of tunnels below the house. She began to wriggle along the stone floor, trying to discover anything she could. There must be a way out! What would a spy do? Feeling tears roll down her face, she had to fight not to lose herself to deepest alarm; little good that would do her now!

The pain in her head stole her breath away and she fell back against the wall to steady herself. If she could not clear her muddled wits, she would not be able to find a way out of this dilemma. Loosening the knots was not a quick prospect, so she fell forward onto her knees and slowly began to crawl around the room. Determining where she was would help her plan what she could do, if anything, to escape. Giving in to her fears was not an option. She could see nothing, the darkness being absolute, she tried to use her other senses. Her prison was made of stone walls and floors, and it smelled similar to the wine cellar at Hawthorne Abbey. There was no sound but her ragged breathing.

When she reached another wall, she found no exit; nor was there a fairy godmother to conjure a door to safety. The exertion needed to traverse the room with hands and feet bound was exhausting. She paused to rest, and biting her lip against the chafing, once more worked to ease the knots at her wrists. Her breathing was rapid with fear. Could there not be a tiny bit of light or air? Was that too much to ask?

She could not keep her thoughts from growing morbid as she tried and tried in vain to free herself. Why had someone done this to her? Had her aunt discovered she was helping Wellington and was punishing Amelia for her betrayal?

No, she refused to think Aunt Lisette capable of such duplicity, even though Amelia herself was committing the same. A horrible guilt assailed her. Using the wall, she managed to hoist herself up to a sitting position; the pain in her head caused by the movement made her retch violently. The sheer force with which she was sick left her too weak to do anything but lie back down and close her eyes.

Sometime later, Amelia awoke with a start to the feel of water touching her face. She opened her eyes. The smallest amount of grey light was creeping into the prison from somewhere above her. It was still difficult to make anything out, not least because the room was spinning about her.

It took enormous effort to keep her eyes open, and she wanted nothing more than to return to sleep, but some instinct warned her that the water around her was getting deeper. Gritting her teeth against the pain, Amelia lifted her head and forced her eyes to focus.

Although it was necessary to squint in order to discover her prison, presently she espied a ladder descending from beneath a small window near the ceiling. Little good it could afford her, she reflected bitterly, with bound hands and feet, when it did not reach the floor.

The water was now flowing over her hands, and she realized she would soon perish from the cold if she did not get above the rising tide. She must be in some sort of cistern! No one would ever think to look for her in such a place. Wriggling her hands in the cold water was becoming harder; she could barely feel her fingers. As she stretched them in an effort to restore some circulation, the fabric binding gave slightly. It had loosened a fraction!

Somehow, she had to get her hands out of the water to warm them. What kind of evil person would leave her to die this kind of torturous death? Would that the blow had killed her! Icy fingers wrapped around her heart at the thought of slowly drowning to death in this hell-hole. Sitting up caused her head to spin and she almost retched again. She had nothing left to vomit, and the feeling slowly eased when she sat still.

It took a few minutes for some feeling to return to her hands. Redoubling her efforts, she was able to loosen the fabric enough to slide her hands to freedom. The knots around her ankles were tougher to loosen, but eventually she was able to toss the binding aside. By this time, the water had risen almost above the tops of her half-boots. Little protection would they provide if the water rose any more, she mused ruefully. Once free, she gingerly felt the back of her head, and found a large indention and sticky, matted hair. She sucked in her breath at the stinging discomfort. Who had hit her? And why?

If she wanted to survive, she would have to reach the window near the ceiling. Looking up at the base of the ladder, she mumbled one of her groom's favoured oaths; it appeared an impossible feat. The only way would be for the water to rise enough to carry her to it—but would she die from the cold before that happened?

CHAPTER 15

*A*fter Philip had followed Tobin and explained the commander's plan, he went to his rooms looking forward to a few hours respite. He was glad to be leaving, for with the death of Lannes, and Pierre plotting some type of coup within the ranks, the danger was very real. Who could say what might happen next, especially with the vitriol Josefina had shown towards Amelia. Thinking of the latter, he decided to stop at her chamber to satisfy himself that she had suffered no ill effects from her experience. It was never easy to see a dead person and especially not when they had met such a violent end.

He rapped softly so as not to disturb anyone nearby—or advertise his clandestine visit in the wee hours of the morning—but the door creaked open with his meagre knock. He frowned and pushed the door fully open, knowing something must be wrong. The lamp still burned bright, and the windows were wide open to the cold night air. He hurried across the sitting room to her bedchamber, but the bed had not been slept in, and there was no sign of Amelia. He peered inside the dressing room, but there was no sign of her there, either. He walked back into the sitting room and paced the floor, trying to think. Perhaps she had gone back to console her aunt, but it looked as

143

if she had been disturbed while painting. There was a streak of paint running across the canvas, which appeared to otherwise be complete. He knelt down, to find a cloth and paint brush had fallen carelessly on the carpet along with splashes of red paint. Thoughtfully, he touched the fresh paint; something about its consistency made him bring his hand up to his nose to smell it. The sticky substance had the telltale metallic odour. It was blood—and Amelia was in trouble. He ran at once to awaken Waverley and Wellington. If the blood was hers—if she were badly hurt—then time was of the essence. Abruptly, he discovered a professional detachment was hard to maintain.

As he waited for Waverley and Wellington to dress, he went back to Lady Amelia's rooms to see if he could discover any clues. He looked around the room and found a candlestick, heavily stained with blood, under the edge of a chair.

"What has happened?" Waverley demanded, entering the room while still donning his coat. Wellington was not far behind.

"It appears as though Lady Amelia has been harmed. I found blood on the carpet and this candlestick. The evidence points to her having been attacked while she was painting. He showed them the streak of paint across the canvas and where her brush had fallen on the floor.

"Good God!" Waverley exclaimed.

"Who the devil would do such a thing to a young lady?" Wellington looked ready for a battle royal.

"I believe I know who may be responsible, but first we must find Amelia. She could be gravely injured. I will search the room for hidden passages. It would not be easy to take a limp body through the window. Also, the risk of being seen, either in the hall outside or elsewhere in the house, would be great, although not impossible," Philip said.

"I will look in the hall," Wellington announced.

"Here is a servants' door," Waverley said as he opened a panel in the wall. "Our servants come and go through a similar entrance. I will investigate this stairway. If she was bleeding, I imagine there will be a trail."

Philip nodded and began to search for secret passages in the walls and hidden trap-doors like the one in his rooms. If he were going to kidnap someone here, he would use the tunnels. "Shall we meet in the courtyard when we have finished searching?" he suggested as the two other men departed.

If this was due to Josefina, Philip snarled to himself, he would be hard-pushed not to strangle her. How dare she do such a thing!

At this moment, he could easily allow himself to panic but his training stood him in good stead and he was able to concentrate on the task at hand. There was no hidden trap-door in the floor beneath her rooms, and he was glad of it. Imagining her thrown into one of those dank, dark cells to bleed to death made his blood run cold. Nor did he find any sign of a secret passage in the walls, so he took up a lamp and followed Waverley through the servants' door in the wall. He strongly suspected Pierre or Josefina would have used that route rather than the main halls where they might be observed by guests. No servant would be awake by choice at two o'clock in the morning.

A few drops of blood were scattered along the floor, and there was another large smear of it on the wall near a doorway, where the assailant would have had to use a hand to open the door. Waverley was nowhere in sight, so Philip trod onwards in the direction of what he assumed must be the kitchen. In his heart, he knew that Josefina had done this, but had she acted alone? It would have been a hard task for Josefina to bear Amelia's weight by herself. Where could the wench have taken Amelia?

The passage came out in the flagged corridor by which he had reached the kitchen earlier that night when he had seen Pierre. Turning into it, he recognized the maid's door and paused outside, debating whether or not to confront her. If she could be convinced to help, he deliberated, Amelia might be saved. He knocked and waited, but there was no answer, so he opened the door. The small room was empty.

He cursed, and hurried towards the courtyard. Waverley and Wellington were already there, waiting.

"Anything?" he asked.

Wellington shook his head.

"I found a trail of blood which led to the kitchen, and then it stopped," Waverley added. "I imagine they went outside."

"I followed the trail as well, since there were no hidden passages in her room. I think one of the maids, or her brother, did this. I overheard the wench speaking with her brother, who turned out to be the man who tried to attack Amelia and I on our way here. I left him bound, but not injured."

"Revenge?" Waverley asked.

"He all but confessed that he had killed Lannes, and she expressed jealousy of Amelia. She has been my contact this year past, and recognized me."

"This is a far deeper game than I had thought," Wellington remarked gravely. "They may have decided to harm Lady Amelia in order to weaken Madame Lisette. If I understand the situation, it seems that Pierre killed Lannes in order to gain power in the hierarchy."

"It would appear so, as best as I can tell," Philip agreed. "The maid is not in her room—I looked. We must act swiftly."

"Where could she have taken her?" Waverley asked.

"I wish I knew. We need Tobin. Waverley, can you send your man to fetch him from the village? He might be able to help better than anyone. He knows his way around the tunnels and is sweet on the maid. He might be able to find her," Philip said.

Waverley nodded and left at once.

"I will wake Madame. This is not a matter to keep secret. We need everyone searching, now," Wellington declared.

Philip nodded and hurried to his apartments and the hidden access to the tunnels. He knew not the other entrances from inside. At this point, Amelia could be anywhere, and in the dark, it would be an almost impossible task to find her. They could have abandoned her in a cell or even thrown her in the ocean. At the thought, he swallowed deeply. What was their intent? It was hard to fathom jealousy as a motive. Nevertheless, it was a powerful emotion and Philip had seen grown men duel to the death because of it. He had to find her—it was unbearable to think of life without her vibrancy in it.

Amelia was a light in the darkness and the earth would be dim without her. He knew he was acknowledging something deep inside which he would have to deal with later, but *first* he had to find her alive.

Running down the hundred or so steps in the cold, damp darkness, he prayed for her to fight and not give in to the fear and sickness she must be feeling. He would find her—he had to.

When he reached the door to Madame's office, he began to yell, hoping the guards would come to his aid.

Madame would be there shortly, he was sure, but he could not wait.

The guards came running at the sound of Philip's shouts. Quickly, he explained who he was and the situation, and they dispersed to search the tunnels. Philip knew not where to look and was afraid of becoming lost himself. Desperate to do something, he went out the cave opening to the rocks to see if he could signal Captain Frome. He feared the Captain may no longer be in support on the water since Wellington had called a halt to the operation. He signalled anyway, and waited. If someone was out there, he needed to know if they had seen anything.

As he waited, he could hear the sounds of the search taking place as the sound of boots and shouts echoed through the stairwells and tunnels. By now, the entire household would surely be awake and searching.

Philip could see a boat approaching, but as it came nearer, he could tell it was not the Englishman. Philip was desperate, however, and when the fishing vessel was close enough to hail, he explained what had happened and who they were looking for. The fishermen agreed to inform the castle guards immediately if they found anything.

Philip returned to Madame's office; still attired in her dressing gown, she had evidently not waited to dress and was pacing the floor, looking distraught.

"Captain Elliot! Have you found her?"

"No, not as yet. I hope you do not object, but I have sent your guards to search. I do not know the area well enough."

"I am grateful that you thought to do so. Who would want to hurt Amelia?"

"I am not certain, but I overheard a man bragging to one of the maids that he had killed Lannes. I believe his name is Pierre."

Madame gasped and covered her mouth with her hand. She looked dishevelled, and Philip felt a small measure of sympathy for the woman.

"I think he may have tried to hurt Amelia in order to upset you, but I can only guess what his motive might have been. Do you know of any wrong-doing linked to Pierre that might give us a clue?"

She shook her head as if disillusioned. Tears streamed down her face.

"Unless he is seeking a ransom, how would harming her benefit his cause?" she cried. "She has nothing to do with our greater purpose."

Relapsing into silence again, she took a turn about the small room. "He and Lannes disagreed on how to run our operation. Pierre was always trying to usurp my authority and, in turn, that of Lannes."

"Where does Pierre live? Perhaps we could search his home."

Two of the guards rushed into the office dressed in plain uniforms with dark coats and tan trousers, a rifle strapped across their chests. "There is nothing to be found in the prison cells, Madame," they reported.

"Thank you," Madame said. "Please go and assist the others in searching the tunnels."

"*Oui, Madame*," they answered and hurried away.

"Wellington and Waverley were intending to search the house, but I do not believe she is there. I sent some men to look in the village since Wellington informed me the trail of blood ended in the kitchen." Her voice cracked as she said the words.

"We need to find Pierre and the maid. I fear time is critical to Amelia's chances of survival."

Wellington entered the office as Philip spoke. "There is no sign of Lady Amelia in the house. Have you fared any better?"

"No, sir. We were just discussing the need to find Pierre and a maid, Josefina, who is his sister, by all accounts. It seems probable she gave him access to the house."

"Their family has a farm outside the southern gate to the fortress," added Madame, having composed herself. "I will take you there myself. Pierre has much to answer for." Her voice was laced with ice.

They climbed the stairs to the house in silence. They found Waverley trying to console the Duchess. "Have you found anything?" she asked when they entered the drawing room.

"*Non, ma chérie.* My men are searching the tunnels, but my instinct tells me she is not there. They would have been seen by the guards if they had taken her there. I will return momentarily. I need to change into riding attire." She hurried away and they continued to deliberate where Amelia could be.

"As there been any sign of Lieutenant O'Neill?" Philip asked.

"No. My man has not returned, either," Waverley answered.

"Perhaps he had a notion of where they might be and went after them. Do you stay here, in case there is any word, and we will search outside."

The Duchess said nothing but Waverley nodded his agreement.

Madame returned, wearing a white riding habit in the military style, and they went to retrieve their waiting mounts from the groom. Madame was silent. Dawn was beginning to break over the horizon, making their path easier to follow.

Philip scanned the area for any signs of the kidnappers or their victim. He was feeling more desperate as each minute passed. It had perhaps been two or three hours since he discovered Amelia was missing, and he knew it was likely they did not have many hours left to find her alive. The air was thick with moisture and drops of rain began to fall from the sky. Madame cursed with uncharacteristic heat and urged her horse along a rough track towards Pierre's small farm. When they arrived in front of the white farmhouse, Madame dismounted without waiting for help and marched up to the front door. She pounded on it angrily as Philip and Wellington exchanged surprised glances.

The door opened after a few minutes, to reveal Pierre in a dishevelled state. Philip and Wellington dismounted and, in silent accord, moved closer in case they were needed.

"Madame?" Pierre's voice held evident surprise.

"Where is my niece?"

"I do not know."

Philip believed him. It was difficult to feign that kind of innocence.

"I know what you did to Lannes." She pulled out a pistol and pointed it at him. "I want to know what you did with my niece. We can discuss why later—if I let you live."

Pierre held up his hands. "I swear on my life, I did not hurt your niece."

"Then tell me where Josefina is."

"I left her in her room, with her lover, a few hours ago. I have not seen her since."

"I think he is telling the truth," Philip said quietly. "I saw him leave the fortress alone... unless he returned, of course."

"Your sister is not in her room. Where would she go if she was in trouble?"

The rain, which had been increasing steadily, began to pour down, and the horses were growing restless as the driving shards saturated their fine coats.

Madame cocked her gun and raised it closer to Pierre's chest.

"Since she had a lover with her, I can only suppose she would go to him," Pierre offered sullenly after a pause.

"You will dress and go looking for her at once. If you can find my niece alive, I will let you live."

Pierre nodded, clearly believing Madame meant what she said.

"I will stay with him," she announced, turning to Wellington.

"I believe I know where her lover is billeted in the village. I spent some time here after I was washed ashore from the shipwreck." Philip spoke casually, knowing Madame was eyeing him closely. What did she think had happened to him? He could only conjecture.

Wellington decided to take charge of proceedings. "I will return to the tunnels, discover what the guards have found, if aught, and then lead them in a search of the grounds if they have not found her."

Philip went to the house where he had lived and climbed the steps to his rooms. Knocking on the door, he yelled Tobin's name. He would be furious if he found the rogue still abed when they needed him so desperately.

There was no answer, so Philip opened the door. He knew from experience that the latch was worthless.

CHAPTER 16

*P*hilip entered the apartment. It was dark inside. Finding a lamp, he and lit it—there was no one there. The bed had been slept in, however, and it appeared as though Tobin had left in a hurry.

"One can but hope he is out searching for her," Philip muttered. "But where? Where are you, Amelia?" he asked desperately of no one as he left Tobin's rooms and headed back towards the fortress to continue his search. His mind kept telling him that people tended to return to what was familiar, so, he thought, if it was Josefina who had done this wicked thing, then it was likely she would have taken Amelia to somewhere between her home and the fortress. The rain was still pouring down in sheets, which made an impossible, worrisome task even more miserable. The sun was beginning to rise, but the blanket of dark rain clouds made it dreary as more storms threatened.

He stopped before a stream and the horse bent down for a drink. Philip used the pause to look around. The water was moving faster than it had been when he had crossed earlier, and it was running away from the fortress. When Scipio had finished drinking, Philip decided to follow the rushing water as it descended beside a path which paralleled the road past the fortress. It was a natural track, which they had also taken on their way to the farmhouse. The water was filling, by way of a ditch, a conduit house positioned between the fortress and the farmhouse. The stone was the same as the cliffs and manor house and covered a subterranean reservoir, into which the water was pouring with great speed. Philip dismounted and tied Scipio to a nearby tree in order to begin searching for the entrance. Since the reservoir was partly buried, it meant there was only one way in and out.

He began to shuffle around the sides of the large water house, wary of the mud and slippery undergrowth surrounding it. The rain was beating into his eyes, and he feared there was no possibility of Amelia being alive if she had been thrown inside. He had to cross the torrent of water gushing into the cistern through an open drain. Losing his footing, he slipped, landing up to his waist in the cold water. The ditch was wide as well as deep and he was immediately drenched. Cursing at his clumsiness, the weather, his misfortune and more alarmed than ever for Amelia, he dragged himself to the other side. Very soon, his teeth were chattering.

There was a rusted door near the top of the water house, and although he released the latch, the door was jammed. Standing on a stone block beneath the door, he propped his boot against the outside of the door and pulled with all his strength. Could she be in there if the door was as difficult as this to open? Could Josefina have opened this herself? Perhaps the rainwater was making it stick. He gave another pull with all his might. The door suddenly gave way; his body weight threw him backwards. Scrambling to his feet, he clambered back up to the opening and peered inside. Water was rushing into the pool below; the sound echoed like thunder around the brick-lined reservoir. Urgently, he searched the darkness for any sign of her.

"Amelia! Amelia!" he cried desperately.

He could not see well enough to determine whether or not she was inside. As he stared helplessly, his arm knocked against something just below the hatch, drawing his attention to an iron ladder. Without stopping to consider, he turned around and began climbing down inside.

"Now, why could you not leave well alone?" a female voice called from the door above.

He looked up. "Josefina?"

"Oh, so you do know me. I knew it was you."

"Where is she?" he demanded in her French tongue.

"Is that any way to speak to someone you want answers from?"

"Did you kill her?"

"I could not say. I have not heard anything from her in some time. Of course, that could be because of the rain."

"Josefina, this is not a game! Amelia could die!"

"So she could. It is too bad, you know. We could have had a nice life together."

"You will not get away with it, Josefina. The whole fortress is looking for her—and you. Even Pierre is looking."

That caught her attention for a moment, and then he could see she made a decision by her changed expression. "You are the only one who knows it was me. Enjoy each other's company!" She straightened and, before he could protest, slammed the door shut. With a morbid note of finality, he heard the latch click into place.

He cursed. He had made a complete mull of that and now he was trapped too. However, it meant Amelia was down here somewhere! Hardly daring to hope, he rushed down the ladder to find her amongst the foul, musty pit of wet and darkness.

When he dropped from the ladder to the floor, the water was above his knees. He held on to the wall and began to skirt the edge of the chamber.

His foot found her first. Dropping to his knees, his heart clenching with fear, he felt for any signs of life. She was sitting propped against the wall, the lower half of her body completely covered with ice-cold water.

Placing his ear close against her nose and mouth, he felt a small breath of air. "Thank God!" he exclaimed aloud, at once scooping her up into his arms. He had not the slightest notion how he was going to save her.

He stared upward, more in hope than assurance. Their only chance of salvation lay up high. Scanty light drifted in through a small window high up in the wall. If only the rain would stop, he might see better. Although he knew it to be futile, he strained his eyes to pierce the gloom. If there were any sort of ledge on which he could lie her; if he could somehow help her to dry, she might have a chance to live. It would be an exceedingly difficult task to carry her up the ladder with her unconscious and her body limp.

As expected, he perceived no such shelf. Slowly, therefore, he began to climb the ladder, holding her as best he could with one arm. Being chilled to the bone himself, he shook with the effort. He had succeeded in clambering up four rungs when Amelia's body began to slip from his arms. Snatching at her arm, he barely managed to keep from dropping her back into the water and, in desperation, leaned against the ladder, wedging her body between his and the rusty iron. Breathing heavily, he said a prayer for strength. There was nothing else left that could help him now. Once his breathing had recovered a little, he pulled their bodies up four more rungs. If Amelia survived, she would be battered and bruised from his meagre efforts, never mind the damage Josefina had done.

"Josefina!" he screamed, his voice echoing through the chamber, in the vain hope she would find some shred of conscience left in her soul and come to save them. He paused again to try and summon the energy to go up the last four rungs. If he could scream and beat on the door enough, perhaps someone else would wander by and hear them or startle his horse enough to break free and send the alarm.

Josefina had to be outside still, listening, and he would try to wear her down. He reached the top of the ladder with his lifeless burden and turned to a position where he could prop himself with Amelia on his lap. He felt the gash on the back of her head, but the bleeding had stopped and a sticky substance came away on his fingers. He hoped that was not a sign of her impending death.

With great care, he balanced Amelia on his leg and stretched up to push at the door, but it would not budge. Their only hope was for someone to open it.

He took his knife and opened it for longer reach before banging the hilt against the iron door. At the noise, Amelia stirred a little in his arms and his heart leapt with joy.

"Forgive me, my dear, but noise is our only hope."

Her eyes opened just a fraction and she gave either a small grimace or smile.

"Philip," she tried to say.

"Yes, it is I. Stay with me!"

She did not; her head slumped back into unconsciousness, and his despondency grew.

Pausing only to switch arms and readjust his burden, he continued to bang on the door, alternating with yelling for Josefina. It felt like hours that he laboured thus. The water below continued to rise, but he no longer heard the rain beating a tattoo on the metal door overhead. It gave him a small glimmer of hope. Reaching upward to bang on the door yet again, he heard voices.

"Josefina! What are ye doing out here, lass?"

"Tobin!" Philip recognized the voice, and with renewed zeal began to bang on the door as hard as his waning strength would allow.

"Leave it, it is not your affair!" Josefina called.

"I cannot do that, lass. Someone is stuck in the cistern," Tobin said. His voice sounded closer.

"Tobin! Help!" Philip called.

"Do not open that door!" Josefina ordered angrily.

"Ouch! Why did ye hit me, lass?" Tobin yelled.

Philip strained to listen as they argued, but the sounds were muffled. Philip said a prayer that Tobin would hold his own. Josefina had grown desperate and would not hesitate, he was convinced, to kill Tobin too. Hopefully he was on his guard now that he knew what she was capable of.

The sounds changed from arguing to grunting and scuffling; something banged against the door a time or two, and Philip knew not what could be happening. His body was gripped with anxiety and he could no longer feel his toes. At last the latch lifted on the door, but apparently their rescuer was having difficulty with it as well. It was another minute or two before the rusted hinge creaked and the sky beckoned above them, and then Tobin's face appeared over the hole.

"I never thought I would be so pleased to see your face, Lieutenant."

"Nor I yers, Captain."

"Help me to lift Lady Amelia out. She is very ill and I am afraid I cannot, at the moment, feel my legs."

"Aye. Let me call fer help." Tobin's face disappeared and then Philip heard a loud whistle, evidently to call the other searchers to their aid.

Presently, Tobin again bent over the opening, his arms stretched out, and Philip did his best to lift Amelia upwards. He was not certain Tobin would be able to lift her from that distance, but once he had his arms under her, it eased the burden on Philip's legs and he was able to provide the final push needed to get her through the door.

A cavalcade of guards and servants arrived soon afterwards to aid in the rescue. Philip was pulled from the cistern and collapsed on to the ground. His legs stung with the attempted return of circulation and would not support him. Madame galloped up on her milk-white horse and directed her underlings to carry Amelia back to the house on a litter. Philip kissed the ground in gratitude.

"I almost doona want to ask how ye were so daft as to be locked in the hole with the lady," Tobin said.

Philip cast a quelling look at the Irishman. "Your *bonnie lass* was hiding, then shut the door behind me when I went down to find Lady Amelia. Where is Josefina now?"

Tobin sighed and inclined his head to the left. Philip looked up to see the maid trussed like a Christmas goose and being hauled away by the guards.

"'Tis a cryin' shame," Tobin said wistfully as he touched the darkening bruise on his right eye. "Such a bonnie lass to be short a shilling."

Amelia could hear voices around her, but her head throbbed and was spinning, making it too painful to contemplate opening her eyes. Using her other senses, she tried to orient herself. She was cold, yet she burned with fire. Was such a thing possible? What had happened to her? She strained to hear the voices around her, some of it was French. She was in France. Memories flashed before her closed eyelids—her aunt's face, her own assignment with Philip. *Philip*. He had saved her. He had held her tenderly and whispered sweet reassurances in her ears while simultaneously making the loudest noise that had grievously hurt her head.

"Did she move?" she heard her sister say.

"M, m, m..." She tried to say Meg but it came out as a moan.

Someone squeezed her hand. "She is still so cold! Are you certain she is warm enough?"

"Send for more blankets," Waverley ordered.

Amelia tried to open her eyes, but the light was blinding. She immediately shut them again.

"Thank God you are awake!" Meg exclaimed, leaning forward to kiss her cheek.

"Shut the curtains so the light does not hurt her eyes," Waverley said to someone. His tone made it a command. "There now, Amelia. You may try to open your eyes again."

She opened them slightly, and was able to see a little, but the light made her head hurt. A maid came with more blankets and put hot bricks under the covers. Her legs and feet felt very painful.

"What happened?" she whispered with difficulty. Her voice was hoarse and her mouth dry.

"All in good time. Would you like to try some tea?" Meg asked.

Amelia nodded slightly, but she regretted the movement.

She sipped the tea at first and then gulped as though she would never drink again. It was a taste of heaven. When the cup was pulled away empty, she frowned.

"Philip. Is he unharmed?" she asked, not realizing she had used his Christian name.

"He is resting. You were both cold and wet for several hours, but you, my dear, had lost a great deal of blood."

"He will be well?"

"He only suffered cold and exhaustion. He did not receive a blow on the head, nor lie in a wet cistern all night."

"Is that what happened? May I have more tea, please?"

Waverley took the cup and refilled it while the Duchess stroked her brow.

"Yes. If Captain Elliot had not thought to come and tell you of our plans to leave..." She broke off, choked by sobs. Waverley came up behind her and put his hand on her shoulder.

"One of the maids took it into her head to dispose of you. Philip is blaming himself, but she hit you in the back of the head with a candlestick—we think when you were painting—somehow dragged you down the path and threw you in the cistern," Waverley explained.

"I remember being in the cistern." Amelia swallowed. "My hands and feet were bound and my head hurt so badly."

"I am sorry your head hurts, but if not for the trail of blood, we might not have found you in time."

"I should let the doctor know you have awakened. He said if you woke soon, there was good reason to be hopeful for a full recovery." Waverley left the room.

"You should continue to rest, my love. I do not wish to delay your recovery," Meg said.

"When you see Captain Elliot again, please tell him I wish to see him."

"Very well. He will be greatly pleased to know you are awake."

Amelia was left alone to lie in the warm, comfortable bed and think. She had very nearly died. Such an experience made one take stock. What really mattered to her now? She had come here to meet her aunt, but also to endeavour to learn if there was to be another plot to overthrow the King.

Both of those goals had been accomplished, but for Amelia they could not coexist harmoniously. She cared for her aunt, and she thought her aunt cared for her, but she could not allow Lisette to lead another uprising against Europe—if that was what she indeed had planned.

It was some comfort to know her aunt had not ordered her harmed. She could almost forgive the maid her jealousy, even, though Philip had made neither of them promises. Yet was it simple jealousy that had caused the maid to act? Amelia might never know the answer to that.

The door to her rooms opened, and she saw her aunt look in.

"Meg said you were awake. I needed to see for myself." She walked into the room, dressed all in black. It made her look like a different person—both aged and forlorn.

"Yes. It seems I had a fortunate escape."

"How do you feel? The doctor was very concerned about the blow to your head."

"I do not remember being attacked, but I feel the effects." She reached up and carefully felt her head, which was bandaged; the feeling was just beginning to return to her hands.

"This should never have happened. I should have known I did not deserve to have such goodness in my life."

"That is not true!" Amelia insisted, and then regretted the action. She squeezed her eyes tightly closed against the pain.

"Forgive me. Do not excite yourself. I can see what it costs you."

"No one could have known what the maid would do."

"Nor her brother," Aunt Lissette said softly, clearly still affected by the death of her man.

"Is it worth it, Aunt?"

Lisette shook her head, fighting back tears and unable to answer.

"You could return to England with us. You need not fight for this cause anymore."

Aunt Lisette reached forward and took Amelia's hand. "I thank you, truly, but my life is here."

"What will happen to you if you are caught?"

"Then I will die fighting for something I believe in." She sighed heavily and leaned back, releasing Amelia's hand. "Do not worry for me. This is not your battle to fight. Take your beau and return to England and live the life you were meant to live."

"He is not my beau," Amelia confessed quietly.

"I think you are mistaken. I see the way you look at each other when you think the other is not aware."

Amelia's eyes widened at this revelation.

"*Oui, ma chérie.* I do not think you have anything to worry about. 'Tis how your father used to watch your *maman.*"

Amelia instantly felt enormous guilt wash over her. "I came here under false pretences."

"I know why you are here."

"You do?" Amelia braved a glance at her aunt's face.

"I was never under any illusion as to why you were here. It did not matter to me. I have nothing to hide from you, or Wellington for that matter."

"I confess I am relieved. It was not the only reason I wanted to come."

Aunt Lisette smiled sadly at her. "I am happy to hear that. Much of what they say about me is true, though—I am hardly worthy of your consideration."

"Please do not say such a thing! It is not too late!"

Aunt Lisette held up her hand. "Let us not spend the little time we have left together arguing our differences."

"Are you still sending me away?"

"It is for the best, chérie."

"There is nothing I can say?"

Lisette shook her head. "I must see this finished."

Amelia turned her head away. There was nothing left to say. They remained there in silence for a few more moments before her aunt rose quietly and took her leave.

Amelia could not control the tears that streamed down her face. It was grief of a different kind from losing her mother. It was a conscious betrayal, and Amelia knew what her aunt was doing was wrong. There were better ways to fight for what you believed in. Was Amelia herself to leave and do nothing?

There was much on her mind, but it hurt too much to deliberate upon these life-altering decisions when the details were not clear. Deliberate she must, however, yet when her head did not feel as if it was being split with a hammer and when the pull of sleep was not drawing her under.

CHAPTER 17

*P*hilip had slept like the dead—having collapsed from exhaustion once he was able to rest. Amelia was in the hands of the doctor, and there was a little more he could do for her now. Wellington was in a hurry to return to England and the Waverley party was trying to determine how soon Amelia could leave. Philip had great respect for his commander, but it went against every bit of his instinct to go home and leave Madame unguarded and the supplies untouched.

He was frustrated with these games of strategy the two sides were playing with each other. Quite frankly, politics was something Philip abhorred. He had never been privy to the upper echelons of the decision making and favours that went on in the King's circle, but he did believe in the free society in England, and protecting that future for his family. It was something which mattered deeply to him, for that unborn child Adelaide was growing inside her—and for his own children? Was that possible? This was the first time he had allowed for that possibility. First, however, this rebellion must be stopped. For as long as Bonaparte was alive, there was always a chance of further trouble. What, he wondered, was going on within the ranks of La Glacier's organization? What would happen as a result of Lannes's death? Would she rethink her tactic, after what had happened to Amelia?

There was a knock on his door, interrupting his conjectures. "Enter," he said.

"Excellent. You are awake," Waverley said as he entered the room and closed the door. He walked over and took the chair opposite Philip, who was still in his dressing gown, drinking coffee.

"Are you suffering any ill effects?"

Philip shook his head. "I was not sodden too long. I have some pain, but the doctor does not anticipate any permanent damage."

"I am pleased to hear it. You will be happy to know that Amelia is awake. She has asked to speak with you."

"That is good news, indeed. I was afraid—did not know—if she would...awaken."

"None of us knew. She still suffers a great deal of pain, but appears to have her faculties intact."

"Did the sawbones say—will she be damaged from the cold?"

"It is likely there will be some damage to her feet. The doctor has applied poultices and bandages, and is keeping them warm. We are hoping for a miracle."

Philip nodded absently. Why Amelia? Why could not Josefina's wrath have been directed at him instead of that beautiful, perfect creature? How she must despise him!

"Wellington is ready to depart for England. He felt he must make haste," Waverley explained.

"Yes, he dropped in and spoke with me not long ago. When do you plan to leave?"

"As soon as Amelia is able. I will speak to the doctor when he returns."

"It could be some time before he wants her moved."

"Unfortunately, it could." Waverley hesitated.

"Is something on your mind, Luke?" They had been friends a long time, and Philip knew something was bothering him.

Waverley looked him in the eye. "I confess, I cannot be easy in my mind about any of this. I understand why Wellington felt his hands were tied and could not act, but mine are not."

"I was just contemplating that very thing when you walked in. What are you considering?"

"Wait until La Glacier leaves for Elba, then burn everything down."

"Will it not be obvious it was us? That would incite war for certain," Philip argued.

"I do not intend to be caught. No building is immune to fire," he reasoned.

"Perhaps not, but how less likely is success when it is in a cave, as the stores are in, hence the name fortress. I want the same thing as you, but I do not want to start a war. We are horribly disadvantaged with most of our good men in America."

Waverley ran a hand through his hair, as was his habit when he was thinking. "She must believe us back in England when it happens. Then she will suspect Pierre or one of the King's men."

"Every part of my being wants this operation destroyed, but it will shatter Lady Amelia."

Waverley blew out his cheeks. "It is why I wish to do it after their aunt is away. I have no intention of destroying the house."

"If we could be certain it would only destroy the war supplies—but with the amount of ammunition sitting in those caves, it would destroy the whole mountain."

"We must consider it, Philip." Waverley was having difficulty keeping his voice down. "If Napoleon or even another were to lead an army against Europe now...the carnage would be unfathomable. You have seen what he has already done."

Philip looked Waverley in the eye. Both of them knew the cost personally.

"If Madame was not here to organize the rebels, would they fall apart?" Waverley asked.

"What are you proposing?" Philip asked.

"I do not know." Waverley threw up his hands in frustration. "I am not suggesting we dispose of her. I would offer her the loophole of living in England under my protection, if she would have it."

"If it could be so simple."

"Think on it. We do not need to make a decision this moment, although I am anxious to escort Meg home."

"I could stay with Amelia while you return with Wellington. I do not think she is in any more danger from Josefina, and it is clear that Madame Lisette cares for her."

"Meg will not like it, but I will speak with her."

Waverley took his leave, and Philip dressed to visit Lady Amelia. He was uneasy about the entire situation. What if Madame had to choose between Napoleon and Amelia? He thought he knew the answer to that. What if he had to choose between England and Amelia? What a question! He put on a shirt and trousers and in this state of half-dress walked down the hall in his stockinged feet. Stepping gingerly to minimize the pain in his toes, he wondered how much pain Amelia was in. The door was ajar when he reached her chambers and he knocked softly. A maid opened the panel fully and bobbed a curtsy.

"*Mademoiselle* is in the bedroom, *Monsieur*," she informed him.

"Who is there?" Amelia called hoarsely.

Philip walked into the room and was almost brought to his knees by the sight of Lady Amelia lying on the bed, looking frail and helpless. He had thought he was prepared for it—he had held her unconscious in his arms, after all, but seeing her head bandaged and swollen caused him almost to lose his composure. He had to gather himself before he could speak.

"It is I, Philip." He walked to her bedside. "How do you feel?"

She opened her eyes a little, as though it were difficult. "Not fit for a London ballroom, I fear. It will be a few weeks, yet."

He forced himself to smile at her. Even as an invalid, with a bandage around her head, she was beautiful. Her long, red curls spread over the pillow, and seeing them unbound made him long to run his hands through them. He prayed that she would recover and not lose the spirit that made her so captivating.

"And you? Do you have injuries?"

"Nothing of consequence."

"I am glad to hear it. I could not bear to know that you had suffered permanently." She pulled her hand out from under the thick covers and reached for him.

He stepped forward and sat in the chair he presumed the Duchess must have occupied for several hours before Lady Amelia woke up. He took her hand in his. It was so small and fragile, despite the bandages, and the visible skin looked as though it had been burned by the sun.

She was watching him now. "The doctor told Meg I might be disfigured."

"You are alive."

"Yes. Thanks to you. I do not know how to express my gratitude. If you had not found me…" A tear rolled down her face and she turned her head away. "I thought I would die in that dreadful place."

Philip leaned forward and, gently turning her head back, wiped the tear away.

"Amelia." He spoke her name as a caress. "Not finding you was not an option I could entertain. Your being alive is all I need."

She nodded her head slightly and attempted a smile. "What will you do now?"

That was an excellent question, one he could not answer. "I suppose I will await the direction of Wellington."

"Waverley wants to return to England as soon as the doctor thinks it is safe for me to travel," she said, frowning.

"I think that would be for the best."

"Philip, my aunt was here a few minutes ago."

He waited for her to continue.

"She knew everything—why we were here. She was not fooled."

"No. She informed me of that within an hour of our arrival. It was though she was toying with us."

"I do not know what to do. I could not convince her to return to England with me and give up this foolish rebellion."

He stroked her wrist above her bandages, trying to comfort her, yet not wanting to hurt her sore hands.

"I feel helpless in my state, but something must be done! Will you help me?"

Philip was astonished. He had not thought her to be so passionate about stopping her aunt. Why the sudden resolve?

"Lying in that hole, waiting to die, and then waking up with a second chance, made me want to live for something meaningful. If Napoleon and my aunt are successful, thousands of people will die—and for what?"

"If we cannot stop them, I believe you are correct."

"Now that we have this information, I feel it would be wrong not to do something. I had hoped to convince my aunt that she had another choice."

"And she did not choose to cleave to the bosom of her beloved family?" Philip asked sardonically.

"No," Amelia whispered, clearly crushed by her aunt's choice. Philip knew where La Glacier's loyalties were, but he hated to see Amelia hurt.

"If it is any consolation, she does care about you."

"Not enough to undo this atrocity."

"Perhaps not, but all is not lost yet."

AMELIA WAS NOT good at remaining still. She tried to sit up to hear what Captain Elliot had to say.

"You need to remain still!" He leaned forward to try to assist her back down.

"No! I refuse to play the invalid. At least help me sit up."

He gave her a look that indicated he was less than pleased, but he pulled her up gently and the maid helped to prop pillows behind her head. The room spun before her eyes, but she would never admit it to him.

"You may leave us now. I am in no danger from Captain Elliot," she said to the maid who gave a look of disapproval, but obeyed. "Thank you. Now tell me this plan."

Philip went to close the door. The impropriety of it was less of a concern with an invalid than potentially being overheard.

Amelia mockingly raised her eyebrows at him, but expected the effect was lost on him due to the position of the bandage.

He sat back down and moved close enough to whisper. Amelia felt her face flush and she silently cursed her heart's insistence on betraying her head. She had seen no indication from Captain Elliot that he cared for her in the same manner. He had saved her life, of course, but he would have done the same for anyone.

"Lady Amelia?" he asked, looking concerned. "You should rest. This can wait until you are feeling better."

"Forgive me, Captain. I was not attending because I was thinking of something else. Time is of the essence, despite my infuriating head wound, and I will think of nothing else until this is resolved."

Concentrate on what matters, Amelia, she silently chastised herself.

"As you know, Waverley desires to leave as soon as you are able."

Amelia frowned. "That was already the plan."

"I am not yet finished. He moved forward, leaned close to her ear and whispered: "He only wants to pretend to leave, and wait for your aunt to depart for Elba. He then wishes to sneak into the caves and destroy the supplies."

"I want them destroyed, but is that wise? Does Wellington condone it?"

Philip leaned back in his chair. "He does not. He said it is no crime to purchase those things."

"Helping Napoleon escape is, though, is it not? And, unfortunately, we saw the evidence with our own eyes of what they intend to do."

"Waverley and I agree with you. I cannot go against my commander's orders, however."

"But I can," she said defiantly, waiting for his objection.

He shook his head." It is too dangerous and you are in no condition to do any such thing. Waverley, on the other hand, thinks he can manage it."

"I do not want Waverley involved. This has become my battle to fight," she insisted. "They are about to have a child and Meg needs him whole. What if something happened to him?"

"I understand your reservations, but what if something else happened to you? The plan has not been fully devised; there are many details to be considered." He paused before adding, "I should let you rest...the sooner you are well, the sooner we may leave."

Amelia did not wish to be left alone, and searched for something—anything—else to keep him there. "What will you do now?" she asked, before he could leave.

"I do not know. Certainly, this situation must be resolved. If and when I can be assured of peace, I might return to Berkshire and become a farmer." He grinned as though the thought was ridiculous and Amelia felt her knees weaken. Having him smile like that would do more to return circulation to her limbs than any poultice the doctor could concoct.

"I think you would make an excellent farmer."

"You do not think the idea ridiculous?"

"No more ridiculous than my becoming a nun," she teased, and they shared a laugh. The pain was severe, but worth it.

"You should laugh more," she told him. "That is what I remembered most about you while you were gone."

"You thought of me?"

"More than I should have done," she confessed. Being hit on the head had apparently loosened her tongue. "I rather took a fancy to you after that, but now I know it was not the real Captain Elliot I had spun fantasies about."

"Are you saying you have no fancy for me now?" The look he gave her made her nervous, for she did not know whether or not if he was toying with her.

"My fancy for you lies now in a different way," she said evasively.

"I am not certain I approve of that answer, but it will do for now." He stood up. "Is there anything I may do for you before I leave?"

"If you would please ring for some chocolate and biscuits?" She smiled impishly. "I have a rather devilish sweet tooth," she confessed.

He stood and rang the bell-pull and quietly spoke to the maid. She bobbed a curtsy and left the room again.

He returned to sit by Amelia's bedside and she gave him a questioning look. "I thought you were leaving?"

He leaned forward to whisper again. "I have a devilish sweet tooth as well, and while I may not be as ill as you, I think some chocolate would have miraculous healing powers for us both."

Could he be less endearing? She felt more pain in her heart than her head, knowing their partnership would soon end.

The maid returned, and set out a service of chocolate and an array of biscuits and rolls for them. Philip went to the trouble of tucking a napkin into the shawl she wore about her shoulders and she hoped he did not notice how the pulse in her throat was speeding wildly. As they ate and drank, he fussed over her like her old nurse would have done, and for a few minutes she was able to forget about the pain in her head and the betrayal in her heart.

"What is this?" the doctor asked, frowning as he came in behind the maid, not waiting to be announced. "I ordered you both to bed with nothing but barley water until I gave further instructions." The small man with greying hair scowled at them over his small, round spectacles.

"Nothing heals like chocolate," Amelia protested, "and my head feels better when I am upright."

"I will give you privacy," Captain Elliot said, and to Amelia's disappointment he left the room.

"You will be next, *Monsieur Elliot*," he warned.

He set his bag on the table, then began unwinding the bandages about her feet and removing the poultices, handing them to the maid. The mixture of mint, ginger and other strange smells were strong and caused Amelia to sneeze. When the air hit her feet, a strange tingling sensation prickled and she remarked on it.

"Excellent," he responded as he looked on with obvious satisfaction. "Some of the circulation has returned."

She tried to peer over the blankets in an attempt to see her feet. " Only some?"

"Blisters have formed in other places, and we will not know the extent of tissue damage until the blister heals—or the tissue dies."

He took out a long, sharp instrument and poked at her feet and toes, and then her hands and fingers, to see where she had sensation. She could not feel everywhere he touched.

"Will I lose my feet?"

He shrugged in the careless French manner. "It is too soon to say, but I do not think so. Perhaps some toes, but your sensation appears to be returning."

He began to prepare more of the foul-smelling poultice and reapplied it with bandages; then he asked the maid to call for hot bricks.

"How certain are you?" she dared to question. He looked up and raised an eyebrow at her.

"I have seen thousands of cases with soldiers, and yours is not as severe as it could have been. It is fortunate you were rescued when you were. A few more hours in that cistern..." He did not finish the thought. "Now, allow me to look at the sutures on your head."

"Sutures?"

"You sustained a rather nasty gash to the back of your head. Be not alarmed, your hair will cover it in good time. Now that you have awakened, I suspect you will live—as long as we can keep infection at bay. We will know better in a day or two."

Comforting words. Amelia knew a childish urge to stick out her tongue.

"And then may I return to England?"

"If you are alive, *bien entendu*. Your Duke says he can ensure you will be comfortable on his yacht." The doctor gave another Gallic shrug. "It must be nice to be a duke and be sure of the wind and waves."

He bandaged her head again and having packed up his bag, turned back to her.

"You must stay in the bed and remain still. If not, your head may bleed again."

"And I may die." She could not refrain from saying what he was doubtless thinking.

"*Oui.*" He clicked his heels together and left, leaving her feeling stunned and also wishing she had not asked questions.

CHAPTER 18

*L*ady Amelia was not a good patient. Philip, the Duchess and the Duke did their best to keep her in bed by taking turns to sit with her. To this end, Philip had encouraged an afternoon ritual of chocolate and biscuits, and was now having a harder and harder time convincing himself that they could part without leaving a permanent scar on his heart. It appeared as though Lady Amelia would make a full recovery, for which he was truly glad. Nevertheless, some part of him had wished, perhaps, she would no longer be suited to fashionable London and might wish to be a squire's wife in the country.

On this sixth day of convalescence, as had become his habit, he walked from his chambers to hers for his afternoon delight, as he had come to think of it. He knocked on the door and was shocked when Lady Amelia opened it herself.

"Good afternoon," she said with a wide smile.

He reached out for her, afraid she might fall. "What are you doing out of bed?"

"I have declared myself well," she said defiantly, backing away from him as though to prove she could.

"I am, of course, pleased to see you on your feet, but is it wise to go from invalid to your normal pace in one day?"

"Philip Elliot, you are hardly one to speak. You would not have stayed abed for two days!"

"Perhaps not," he conceded. Stepping forward, he took her arm and led her towards the chairs by the fireplace. Madame had ordered a large fire to be maintained day and night, and orange-red flames danced in the draught from the chimney, giving out a comforting warmth. She sighed, but allowed him to help her sit down. He threw another log on the flames and nodded to a maid, who had entered the room bearing a silver salver.

"We are to leave on the morrow," Amelia announced after the maid had set the tray of chocolate and biscuits down before them and departed again.

"Everything is in place, then?" he asked quietly.

"Waverley just left to make the arrangements. I intend to inform my aunt when she visits me next."

"How long have you been out of bed?"

"Do not dare to nag me."

"Forgive me. I am merely concerned." Philip smiled. It was ironic; now that he acknowledged his feelings for her, she was treating him more like his sister did. He would miss this Amelia terribly; Lady Amelia, regrettably, not as much. This Amelia was the one he could see himself growing old with.

"I have not heard from Wellington," he said, as if it mattered. The plan was to proceed whether or not he gave his consent. "Tomorrow, then?" She was saying very little, suddenly. He did not normally need to force a conversation with her.

"Yes," was her simple reply. She had not touched the biscuits and was not drinking her chocolate.

"What is wrong, Amelia? Are you having second thoughts?" he asked, feeling his brow furrow.

"Of course not!" She looked at him with fiery determination in her eyes.

"Very well, then. What is the matter?"

"I would rather not say. Everything will change tomorrow."

Was she thinking beyond their final act, he wondered.

"Have you heard from Tobin?" she asked.

"He is ready, though I cannot like his participation. If Wellington finds out…"

"He will not," she assured him. "This is personal for Tobin as well."

"I was left for dead by her, myself," he added dryly. "However, it becomes an act of war when one of the King's soldiers is a participant."

"I am not a soldier, and I must see this to the end, Philip."

She stood slowly and rang the bell. "I must pack."

He opened his mouth to protest. Surely she was not yet strong enough.

As though she could read his thoughts, she held out her hand to stop his words. "I need this to be over. I cannot wait any longer."

The maid came in and began packing Lady Amelia's belongings.

"I cannot change your mind, then? His Grace will deal with her in his own way." Philip refrained from saying *the proper way*.

She shook her head. "I know you are bound by your military code of honour, but do you think they care for such things? Would they do England the same courtesy? They do not represent France's legitimate government and are not bound by codes and treaties!"

Her voice rose as she worked herself into a passion. Philip stood up and crossed to her side.

"You know that I agree something must be done, do you not? It is the how and why I cannot condone. You are not yet strong, and I do not wish to see you risk your life. We very nearly lost you not above a week ago." Almost unconsciously, he stroked her arm.

"I have not forgotten. Nor the debt I owe you. Please do not stand in my way."

"Very well." He stood aside and made to leave.

"Philip?" She called after him. He turned back to her and the look she bestowed upon him made him feel as though his heart were being pulled slowly from his chest. Instead of speaking, she shook her head and shooed him away.

Leaving Amelia with a heavy burden on his mind, he almost did not see La Glacier in the hall until he was upon her.

"Ah, Captain Elliot. Finished your afternoon tête-à-tête?

He made La Glacier a stiff bow. "Indeed. Your niece has decided she is well enough to depart."

"Yet you do not agree?"

He inclined his head.

"I wonder, Captain Elliot, that her beau could not persuade her to take a wiser course. How is your suit progressing? I had anticipated hearing a certain announcement by now."

"I did not consider it appropriate to press my suit whilst she was injured, Madame."

"*Non.* Of course not. I wish you luck and happiness back in England. I think you will do very nicely together. Never take her for granted," she added as she walked on.

"I would not," Philip whispered after her. He did not want to think any more about Amelia and their false relationship, so he decided to pay a visit to Tobin.

The walk to the village was good for Philip. He needed time away from distractions in order to think clearly. He desperately needed to disassociate his emotions from the task at hand. Even if he could not actively participate in destroying the supplies in the cave, he could try to make certain Amelia and Tobin remained safe and were not caught. He found the Irishman in his rooms, looking morose and none too pleased to see Philip.

"What can I do for you, sir?"

Philip smiled, despite a slight irritation. Tobin could not quite bring himself to be a good officer and submit to authority it seemed.

"Pining over your maid?"

"Not particularly. She is not worth the effort."

Philip was not quite certain that was the case, but he hoped Tobin could forget the Frenchwoman. It had to feel like betrayal at its worst. At least he had helped to rescue Amelia and his tomfool self from the water house.

"I did not know if Waverley had yet sent word to you, but the plan is to depart in the morning."

"Finally," Tobin said with obvious relief. "This means Lady Amelia is recovered?"

"She appears to be. I wish she would not try to do too much before she is fully well, but she can not be convinced otherwise."

"She probably wants it over and done with. I know I do," he said, picking up a piece of wood he was carving.

"Do you know the risk you are taking by defying Wellington's orders?" Philip asked.

"I am seeing Lady Amelia safe. I am not lighting the torch. I do not imagine you will be waiting far away yerself."

"It is imperative that no one sees us," Philip urged.

"I am aware of the consequences, Captain. It is not right for us to leave those supplies here, knowingly helping the enemy in our future slaughter. Wellington will not be sad to hear they were destroyed."

"No, nor will I, but if this incident starts a war, it will be our heads."

"I rather fancy *my* head," Tobin retorted.

"And I want to make certain not another scratch befalls Lady Amelia."

"That is why I am going. I have no qualms about standing before his Grace and explaining that I was trying to protect her."

Philip nodded reluctantly. "You are certain La Glacier never saw you during Lady Amelia's rescue?"

"Quite certain. It was raining and my hat was down low. I saw her ride away in the other direction with Lady Amelia on the litter. She arrived after I had bound Josefina."

"What has become of her?"

"Last I heard, she was sitting in a cell. Pierre is trying to convince Madame of his loyalty and be allowed to take Lannes's place while she is away." Philip and Tobin shared a mutual look of amusement at the unlikelihood of such a thing. Madame was unlikely to forgive Pierre for his or his sister's betrayal. "Why she has not had them dangling from a tree themselves, I would love to know."

"There is some deeper game here than we are privy to, I imagine. We may never have the answers."

"Mayhap she does not want their disloyalty widely known. I'd wager she has plans to execute justice on the ship."

"A likely course," Philip agreed. "The rest of us will anchor at Dieppe until we receive your signal that all is clear."

Tobin nodded. "I will be ready. I only hope the guards are susceptible to brandy again."

"When the cat is away..." Philip began.

"The mice will play. Aye, I am counting on it," Tobin muttered.

Philip stood. "Godspeed, Lieutenant. I pray I will see you again on this side."

Tobin saluted him smartly and Philip took his leave.

IT WAS an entire week before La Glacier's ship departed for Elba. In this capacity, Amelia could not think of the woman as Aunt Lisette. Had she chosen to give up her cause, then perhaps Amelia could have forgiven her. But Amelia was stubborn too, and she believed what Napoleon was doing was wrong. It would be impossible to live with herself if she did not at least try to stop La Glacier from helping him to escape.

A week of waiting had been a week of healing, though she would have preferred being on land to ship. Feeling much stronger now, she awaited the signal from Tobin with much impatience. Matters had changed between Philip and her since their removal from the fortress and she did not know why.

Amelia needed to have done. If Philip did not want her, then she needed to remove herself from his vicinity. Every look and every smile made her remember those times together over the past weeks. She truly did think she was ruined for any other man.

The signal came late on a cold January evening. Amelia could have burst with the relief she felt. They had been cooped up in their cabins because it was too cold to venture onto the deck in the depths of winter. They avoided going into the town for fear of discovery by one of La Glacier's lackeys. They were not so far from Étretat, after all.

Amelia put on a pair of the thick woollen trousers the servants wore, which her maid had altered for her, along with a coat, hat and a sturdy pair of boots. Besides having a functional costume, it was imperative she not be recognized.

"Are you ready?" Philip asked as the yacht began to sail back to the south.

"As ready as I can possibly be," she said. Her voice was steadier than she felt. They had done nothing but rehearse the plan over and over for the past week.

It was almost as if she were another person going to carry out this undertaking. In looks and in character, no one would ever guess this was the Lady Amelia Blake of London.

Meg and Waverley exchanged tearful goodbyes while they waited on deck; Meg reminiscing of being left in the same manner once before, almost a year past.

The yacht anchored far enough away from the fortress so they would not be seen in case guards were looking. Amelia, Philip and Waverley were lowered into a dinghy, where Tobin was waiting for them, and some of Waverley's crew served as oarsmen to row them to shore.

Amelia was shaking inside as they approached the familiar beach which held so many memories for her. Cowering in fear would do her little good, she told herself fiercely—it was too late to turn back now. Her outer cloak was covered in sea spray and she shivered in anticipation as the face of the cliffs hove into view.

The sea was gentle that night—not foretelling of what was to come, certainly.

Suddenly, Philip's face was before her and he put his hands on both of her arms, which did little to settle her racing heart.

"It is not too late. You can stay with me outside."

She shook her head; her voice was too unsteady to speak.

The boat pulled to a stop and the oarsmen jumped out into the knee-deep water so as to pull the craft to dry ground.

"Wait here," Tobin directed.

"He is going to scout about to discover how many guards there are and determine the best course. Hopefully, he can gather them in one place, away from the supplies and in safety. The lure of a keg of brandy is strong on a cold, quiet night on watch."

"Let us hope it is so."

They waited some time for Tobin to return. Amelia could not say how long, for her nerves were shattered and every second felt an eternity.

"They are all locked in one room, as far away from the storeroom as I could get them, and drunk as wheelbarrows. I will lead the way; Waverley and Elliot will look out behind. Understood?"

Amelia nodded. She would be the one to go into the cave and set the long wick at the back of the cavern where all the ammunition was. Once she was outside again, she was to set fire to the end and escape back to the beach as soon as possible. It seemed simple enough, yet the consequences were untenable. Failure was not an option any of them would contemplate.

It seemed as though every step was an experience which took her out of herself, as though time stopped, awaiting each movement. Tobin led and Philip was directly behind her, giving her false courage for the moment. Soon it would be solely up to her. Waverley and Captain Elliot were to keep watch on the room where the guards were hopefully passing a jolly evening, and Tobin would take her to the final tunnel.

When they reached the room where the guards were, Philip took her hand and squeezed it reassuringly. Amelia made the mistake of looking up into his eyes, barely visible by the little moonlight shining in, but enough to see he cared. It took a great effort not to throw herself into his arms. She stood on tiptoe and kissed him on the cheek before turning and hurrying off with Tobin.

As they walked away, it sounded as though the guards were enjoying the keg of brandy, and Amelia prayed they would be safe so close to the entrance of the beach. The plan was to unlock the door when they exited so the guards would have a means of escape. Amelia could not bear it if she thought they had killed someone unnecessarily.

The further they went, the more the darkness seemed to close in on them. The tunnel floor was uneven; more than once she slipped and lost her footing. Each breath was an effort as the air felt thinner and colder.

Tobin stopped and reached for her hand, as if he knew her inner turmoil. "There are some rough steps here," he whispered, and guided her down them. "Not much further now," he said.

Too soon, they reached their destination.

"I will wait for you here," Tobin whispered. He handed her the long wick, which she would roll out from there and light inside the cave. She crept forward slowly in the dark, having memorized the passage so she would not falter, but her legs were still shaking. With indrawn breath, she ventured forward into the cavern's depths. It was almost over. When the wick ran out, she would be there.

So far, she had only walked about twenty paces. All was darkness and it closed in on her as she advanced further into the depths of hell. There should be a door within the next five strides, but was she even going in the right direction? She looked from left to right but saw nothing and spun around, disoriented. She walked five paces one way, her arms outstretched, but there was nothing there. Panic encroached on her senses; she wanted to scream! She could not see or breathe or think clearly. Crouching down on her haunches, she decided to risk lighting her lamp. Hiding the light beneath her cloak, she looked around.

The cold iron door was exactly where Tobin had said it would be —directly in front of her. Slowly, she released an agonized breath of something which was not quite relief. As quietly as possible, she lifted the latch and opened the door, thankful the well-oiled hinges made little sound.

For a moment, she lost her nerve in the darkness and sought the cold, wet wall for reassurance. It was of little comfort, and she quickly snatched her hand away from the slimy, squashy substance which her gloves did little to disguise. Amelia nearly forgot herself and screamed for Philip. Just in time, she pressed her lips together and swallowed the sound. Convincing herself to move forward, she found that the further into the depths she went, the worse the smell of decaying fish. She had to cover her nose in order to carry on.

"Almost there. Almost there," she encouraged herself. At last, the length of twine, which would serve as the fuse, ran out. She lifted her small lamp to ensure everything was in the right place. After all, if the supplies had been moved, then this enterprise was for naught.

Tobin had not exaggerated. Amelia knew little about what it took to equip an army, but to her inexpert eye, it looked as though all of the men in Europe could be outfitted for some time. It was sickening that her aunt had overseen this!

Seeing the munitions only firmed her resolve that she was doing the right thing. A strange feeling came over her, and she had an uneasy thought—it had all been too easy. Perhaps it seemed so due to Tobin's excellent preparation, she mused, to bolster her faltering spirits. She had reached her goal. Now she merely had to exit the caves and return to the boat.

As she reached the door, she held the lamp up to find her path before blowing it out. She let out a squeal.

"Amelia?"

CHAPTER 19

*A*melia tried not to panic, though the blood was pounding through her ears and it was hard to think. They had discussed what to do if she was confronted by someone, but she never thought it would be her aunt! Her hand had automatically gone to the dagger at her waist and she let it drop.

"I expected someone to come back, but not you," her aunt said, lowering her own blade.

There was little else which could have felt like a knife to Amelia's bruised heart. What an agony of conflicting emotions assailed her!

"I love you, Aunt, but I cannot allow you to destroy what I believe in."

"What about my beliefs? Am I not allowed to fight for what I think is right?"

"What about all the lives that will be lost? Your Emperor left a path of destruction and death across Europe."

"You do not remember the Revolution, niece, but I do. I do not expect you to understand, having come from the very aristocracy we are fighting to abolish," she snapped.

"You yourself come from the same blood as I! Have you ever been oppressed?" Amelia questioned.

"At one point, yes," she answered coldly, glaring at Amelia.

"There is a better way. It need not be thus!"

"Then you will have to take that dagger and plunge it through my heart. I will not let you destroy everything I have worked for!"

Amelia raised her chin, affecting a bravery she did not feel. "Indeed? What, then, will you do with me if I do not? You know I cannot kill you."

Her aunt did not answer for a few moments. "I assume you are not alone. My guards must have been disabled very cleverly for you to have reached this far."

Amelia inclined her head, trying not to give away too much. How could they both escape this situation alive? Amelia feared, if she did not return quickly, the men would come after her and kill her aunt.

"It appears we are at an impasse. You must choose, *ma chérie*,"

"The men will be here soon," Amelia prevaricated. "Why did you not leave on the boat as you were supposed to?"

"Because I knew someone would return to try to destroy the armaments."

"This was not supposed to happen, Aunt. No one was to be hurt! Please—turn around and go back to the house."

Instead, her aunt stepped closer. "I cannot. If you insist on bringing this down, I will burn with it."

"Very well. You leave me no choice." With a calmness she was far from feeling, Amelia took out her dagger and cut a length of rope, from the end of the wick. "Turn around," she ordered.

Her aunt gave her one, long look of betrayal before turning around and presenting her hands.

Amelia took her knife. Why did she not fight? Tears streamed down Amelia's face as she tied several knots, cruelly binding her aunt.

Footsteps sounded in the tunnel, and Amelia knew everything was ruined. She had failed in her intent, and now others would be involved who could implicate England—unless it was a trap and the footfalls belonged to guards. She held her aunt close against her chest and put the dagger to Lisette's throat.

Tobin arrived, still disguised, but no doubt her aunt would not be fooled. His eyes went wide at the sight before him and he began cursing in Gaelic.

"Bring her out," he said, but Aunt Lisette refused to move.

"I will not leave," she answered defiantly. "You must kill me."

"I would like nothing more, *leannan*, but this is not my battle to fight, I have been told." He bent and lifted Madame over his shoulder. "Ye've gone soft, Madame, if ye let her live. I almost think ye've grown a heart."

"Where are you taking her?" Amelia asked.

"To safety. If I put her in a cell, she will be burned."

Amelia needed to retch. Nothing was happening in the way it was supposed to! She followed Tobin back out of the tunnel to where they were supposed to have met, and her aunt glared at her every step of the way. Tobin turned to her.

"Finish what you started, lass. I will see her safely out, ye have my word. Can you find yer way from here?"

She nodded, holding back sobs. After she could no longer hear his footsteps, she turned to where the wick lay at her feet and said a quick prayer that what she was about to do was right.

Removing the tools she needed from her pocket, she struck the flint against the steel, and watched the sparks begin to fly and light a piece of cloth. Kneeling down with the flame, she set it to the twine and watched it catch fire and sizzle a path towards the ammunition. Then she grabbed her lamp, turned and ran as fast as she safely could.

Philip was waiting for her by where the guards were kept and took her hand as Waverley unlocked the door. They ran without speaking until they reached the sandy beach, they were both out of breath. Explosions began to sound, echoing from deep within the stone walls, and Amelia buried her head in Philip's chest. Uncontrollable sobs escaped her and he stroked her hair, at the same time holding her tightly to him.

"We must leave," he said, guiding her back to the boat. Waverley was already there but Tobin was not...and neither was her aunt. They climbed in and sat on the narrow benches, watching in silence as smoke began to bellow from the mouth of the cave. Amelia wished she felt proud of her actions, but her only thought was she had destroyed someone she loved in the process.

The oarsmen pushed the boat out into the water and then climbed in. As they began to row, Amelia cried, "Wait!"

"What is it?" Waverley asked.

"Tobin has A-Aunt!" she stuttered, trying to explain. "She found me in the caves and refused to leave, so Tobin came to look for me and had to carry her out."

Waverley and Captain Elliot looked warily at each other. The exchange of glances was over her head, but she caught it nevertheless.

"Tobin was not to return to the boat," Waverley explained. "He would not bring her here, regardless of what occurred. We cannot take her prisoner."

"I must know she is safe!" Amelia protested.

"You must trust Tobin to see to it. He would hardly harm her after going to such lengths to ensure the guards could escape."

"I suppose so," she answered slowly. She pulled her cloak tighter around her. Suddenly, she began to shake uncontrollably; a raw, melancholy chill had her in its grip and it did not seem she would ever be warm again. They watched the guards pour out of the caves, flames and smoke licking at their backs, while the boat drew farther out to sea.

"What comes next?" she asked, staring at the surreal sight.

"War."

WHEN THEY REACHED THE YACHT, the Duchess's relief at their return was palpable. Lady Amelia explained the confrontation with their aunt, and it was only then Philip realized the extent to which Lady Amelia had been distressed in the cave. The way she had described the matter afterwards, in the boat, it had seemed a quick thing, but now he could only admire her fortitude. The lady's torment was evident and he felt for her and the strength she had portrayed in proceeding with destroying the supplies. Once the Duchess was satisfied with

Amelia's explanations, Philip and his fellow adventurers proclaimed exhaustion, and everyone retired to their cabins to sleep for the sail back to England. Hopefully, most of the journey would be achieved while they slept.

Philip dreaded the goodbye to come in England. He believed Lady Amelia felt some not insignificant attachment to him, as well, but matters had changed between them of late, and he felt it best to sever the connection upon setting foot in their home country. Any affection seemed to have cooled on her side, although he had fallen asleep to the rocking of the boat with her beautiful face filling his dreams. On awakening, Philip was shocked to find the shore of England visible already. Sometimes, after a harrowing assignment, he could sleep almost an entire day, for his body seemed to need the time to recover. Having always been one to enjoy the respite an ocean voyage provided, it occurred to him he could have been a sailor, except he did not enjoy confined spaces for indefinite periods of time.

He dressed and made his way to the deck to watch their landing. It fascinated him how the crew worked together to bring them into the docks as they seemed to know when to push and pull the ropes at just the right time.

"Good morning," Waverley said when Philip joined him at the railing. "I hope you enjoyed a restful night? The sea has been kind to us this voyage."

"I slept like the dead," Philip reassured him. "I trust that means the Duchess is faring well?"

"I dare to hope that period of sickness is over. She has been quite well since we set sail."

Philip wanted to let Luke know of his plans, but he was feeling very uncertain at the moment.

"What are your plans?" he asked instead. "Do you go directly to Waverley Park?"

"That is our desire, of course, but we must consider Amelia. I suspect she needs a repairing lease after all that has occurred during our absence and, of course, what happened to precipitate our leaving. Perhaps Somerton might be the best choice as it is closer to London."

"I suspect the scandal with Wadsworth will have died down, but her return will cause some sensation," Philip remarked.

"No more than your return from the dead! While I hope she will go to the country with us, to be companion to Meg during her confinement, I am not sure she will wish to. What have you planned?"

"I must report to Wellington if he is still here, of course. Then I hope for a period of leave to get my affairs in order."

"Selling out?" Waverley turned to look at him, brows raised.

"I do not think it will be possible."

"Because you fear war or because you fear retirement?"

Philip laughed. "Both! I could not begin to speculate on what my circumstances will be when I return to Berkshire; nor, moreover, on what will happen when Wellington discovers the fire and if Napoleon sees his way to escape."

"I could not undertake to say, to the latter, except that Fielding has hinted you will have a respectable income. If Napoleon escapes and amasses another army, we will all be hard-pushed not to return to fight."

Philip let out a growl of agreement.

"Somehow," Waverley continued, "I was under the impression that you meant to speak with me about Amelia. I know the idea was merely to present the impression of courting, but I do not think Meg and I are wrong in supposing you found a deeper attachment for each other. Am I mistaken?"

Philip hesitated to answer. He looked out over the approaching port and wished he had waited a few more minutes to leave his cabin.

He closed his eyes. "You are not," he said softly. "However," he added before Waverley began drawing up the settlements, "I do not think it is in our best interest to pursue the matter."

Philip could feel Waverley's gaze before he opened his eyes to see the incredulous stare his friend was casting at him.

"Whyever not?" he asked, as offended as Philip might have expected Amelia herself to be.

"Must I spell it out for you, Luke?"

"I suppose you must. I can think of no hindrance to such a union. In fact, I cannot think of anyone who handles Amelia so well as you."

"May I remind you I am a career military officer? Would you have her follow the drum? Even if my circumstances in Berkshire are more handsome than I have reason to expect, it does not make me an eligible parti for the daughter of a Marquess and an heiress."

"You do her a grave injustice, Philip. She cares nothing for that, nor do her sister and I."

"I appreciate your words more than I can express, Luke, but I fear that when she realizes I am no more than a gentleman farmer, she will live her life full of regret."

Luke hesitated. "I cannot speak for her, but I wish you would not give up on her all together. I saw her in London, and while she was the belle of every ball, I did not sense it made her happy. Something to think on." Luke slapped Philip on the back and left him to his conflicting thoughts.

What was he to do? He was not his own man while he held his commission, and while he could see Lady Amelia following the drum now that he had undertaken this operation with her, he did not want to ask it of her. Life on the Peninsula had been one of extremes and horrific battles. It was not what he would wish for his wife and future children, should it ever happen again.

Regardless of his feelings, he and Amelia needed to have a proper farewell. Never before had his assignments required such personal investment and intimacy, nor yet had left such an imprint on him. It truly was a partnership of body, mind and soul. He would not feel the same without her, but he would go on with his life without her.

He had never believed in relationships where someone could not function without the other. It was unhealthy and did not, in his opinion, espouse the tenants of true love. For what good was he if someone else was necessary for him to be complete? No, complementing each other was the highest form of love, not overshadowing. Amelia would never flourish in the shadows. She would understand his work and why he must do it... but would she let him go alone?

"We have arrived at last," Amelia said as she took to the rail beside him, leaning her forearms over it. "It seems a lifetime ago I left England."

"How are you this morning?" he asked carefully.

"It is hard to say. I cannot rest easy until Tobin assures us my aunt is safe, but I will be glad of a few days to convalesce."

"Last night could not have been easy. It almost killed me to wait at the cave's entrance."

"I know it."

He reached over and took her hand in his. "I wanted to tell you how proud I am of what you did."

"Thank you," she whispered. "I wish I knew I had made the right decision."

"Will you go to Waverley Park?"

"I suppose I must."

"What do you wish to do?" He turned her towards him and searched her eyes. Would he propose marriage if she avowed she wished for this life first?

"I do not know. That is the problem. I do not belong anywhere."

"I know how that feels." He released her, though he wanted to pull her into his arms. Had she looked inclined towards his suit, he probably would have asked. "Maybe a time in the country will make all things clear. It is where I intend to go if I can obtain leave."

"To Berkshire, did you say?"

"Yes. Welston is a handsome cottage with a thousand acres of farmland. Modest by many standards."

"It sounds lovely, and it is your home."

"I thought it was lost to me forever." He found his throat thickening with emotion.

"You never did tell me about the shipwreck and how you came to be alive."

A gust of wind whipped against the ship and some of Amelia's red locks blew into her face. He brushed them away tenderly and scooped them behind her ear.

"'Tis a time best forgotten."

"I should like to hear it all the same, when you are ready."

"There is little to tell. The ship was intended for the West Indies. Madame sabotaged it with cannon fire, not far off the coast where we departed. When I came to, I was lying on the beach near your uncle and several of the crew members. They were all dead."

"And you were the only one to survive?"

"As far as I know, yes."

"How horrible!" she exclaimed. "And you lived in the village nearby and spied on my aunt the entire time we thought you missing?"

"Yes. I informed Wellington, of course, and he thought it best if she thought me dead. I therefore assumed the role of *Monsieur Lefebre*, pedlar, delivery man, jack of all trades."

"And you bewitched the maid, Josefina."

Philip bowed slightly.

Amelia said nothing as the crew brought the ship into the harbour and secured it with ropes to the posts at the dock. As their trunks were unloaded and carriages came to take them away, they remained next to each other, not wanting to part.

When it could no longer be put off, Amelia turned towards him. "Will you go back?"

"If needs be."

She had one last opportunity to give a sign, any sign, of her desire to be with him.

Instead, she nodded and appeared to force the smile she gave him. Standing on tiptoe she kissed his cheek and whispered in his ear:

"Goodbye, Philip. I will never forget you."

He pulled her into an embrace and held her tight, memorizing everything about her—as if he could ever forget—but the feel, the smell, it would have to do.

Releasing her, he stepped back and made her a regal bow. He could not bring himself to say words of farewell.

"Will you write to me?" she asked, as she placed one boot on the gangway.

"I will," he assured her before turning away to hide his pain.

CHAPTER 20

A few weeks had now passed at Somerton. Amelia had travelled up and down the scale of emotions—from grateful to be alive to the depths of despair—over betraying her aunt and losing Philip. Was it wrong of her to long for a more exciting life? At the moment, the quiet, domestic rhythm of the country, without news or action, felt like a penance. Was that really true, however? Was she merely longing to follow the drum because of Philip? If she were being honest, the answer was yes. Accepting defeat was not something Amelia was good at doing gracefully.

Meg was soon to have a child, and instead of pining in her room any longer, Amelia resolved to be a good sister. Eventually, she hoped, she might one day be able to forget and find a measure of contentment. It was ironic she had spent the last year dissatisfied with all her suitors because of who she had thought Philip Elliot was. Now she was in love with the real gentleman and she could not have him either!

She donned her riding habit of thick, grey wool and made her way downstairs. Winter was still in full force this February, but it was dry and milder than those of her youth at Hawthorne Abbey had been. France would be lovely now, she thought before chiding herself. Why must she add torture to her load by reflecting on the past?

Riding was one of the few occupations she could get lost in and not mope, and she had gradually worked up to long rides as she recovered from her injuries.

"Amelia? Is that you?" Meg's voice questioned as Amelia passed her sister's sitting room.

"Yes. I was going for a ride," she answered, stopping at the doorway.

"That is all you ever do of late. Should we return to London? Would that make you happy?" Meg's face was drawn with concern.

Amelia gave up and went to sit on the chair near Meg. "I do not think it matters where I am, sister. Forgive me for disturbing your tranquillity."

"I am only worried about you—as is Luke. If there is anything we can do to help?"

"You cannot mend what is broken in me, unfortunately. Perhaps I should return to London so you will not worry."

"Do not be ridiculous! I would worry even more if you were not here."

Amelia smiled despite herself.

Luke entered the small room, holding some letters, and went over to kiss Meg on the forehead before squeezing himself onto the sofa next to her.

"Good morning, ladies. Off for a ride in this cold?" he asked Amelia.

"Of course she is," Meg retorted.

"Indeed? Long hours in the saddle remind me of my days on the Peninsula."

"Luke, don't," Meg warned.

"It is of no moment, sister. There is no use in pretending he does not exist. My heart will recover in time."

Luke looked at Amelia thoughtfully. "I try not to interfere in my friend's amours, and you know I have wanted to let you choose your own helpmate."

"But?" Amelia prompted.

"But I think perhaps you both need a nudge in the right direction."

"I cannot throw myself at him!" she protested. "Well, no more than I already have," she added sardonically, feeling her cheeks burn at the admission. How bold she had been, away from the restrictions of London!

He set his letters down on his lap. "Philip and I had a discussion on the ship, before we arrived. It is obvious he cares for you."

"As she does for him," Meg added—unnecessarily, Amelia thought.

"Do go on," she said cautiously.

"I did not want to interfere, but he did not feel he could offer you the life you deserved. Marrying him, he said, would mean either following the drum or that of a gentleman farmer. I think, if he had perhaps had some encouragement and reassurance in that direction, he might have taken the chance."

"What more encouragement could I have given?"

"It appeared to me that you had become good friends after your injury. Mayhap he felt you thought of him as a brother?" Meg suggested.

"I cannot believe we are having this conversation! Had any of our friendship occurred in England, we would have been wed by special licence as soon as the ink was dry." She stood and began to pace about the room.

"Shall I demand satisfaction of him?" Luke queried with a twinkle in his eye.

"I do not wish to be married by force, thank you," Amelia snapped.

"I would not shirk my duties, you know," he added.

"Luke, is that letter from Tobin?" Meg asked, leaning over his shoulder and thus neatly changing the subject.

He looked down at the open sheet of paper. "She has done it, by Jove!"

"Who has done what?" Amelia stopped and asked.

"La Glacier has escaped, and Tobin believes she is already at Elba, or if not, soon will be."

Amelia sank onto a chair and buried her face in her hands. "Was he holding her captive?"

Luke read more of the letter. "Not precisely," he answered. "He removed her to the house and stayed with her whilst we made our escape."

"So she was unharmed?" Amelia collapsed back into the chair with relief.

"Yes, it appears our endeavour was successful in that regard. However, once her guards discovered what had happened, they quickly came searching for her, and Tobin had to escape also."

"Was there a great deal of damage?"

Luke paused and read on, frowning. "There were some collapsed tunnels from explosions. He heard rumours that Pierre and Josefina perished in their cells, which he takes responsibility for."

Amelia felt numb. No matter how spiteful Josefina had been, she would not have wished the girl murdered in turn.

"Tobin says he did his best to follow La Glacier, but the fortress is now deserted. The groom he had befriended is now in the village and says she left for Elba to exact revenge."

"Oh, dear," Meg whispered.

"'Tis no less than I expected," Waverley said, dropping the letter into his lap.

"What now?" Amelia asked. "I feel I should do something."

"I am surprised I have not heard anything. I will ride into Town to discover what I can." Luke was still involved with the Foreign Office and the Lords, though he no longer wore a uniform. "Wellington is back on the Continent, so is probably aware of the circumstances."

"I made a mull of things." Amelia felt ill. She had handled things poorly with her aunt, and had considered, over and over, how she could—should—have contrived differently.

"You must not think of it that way. I had to learn that myself whilst in the army. You can only control so much, and you controlled what you could. In fact, I would argue you went well beyond what was asked or expected of you...certainly a young lady."

"Thank you," she said softly, but her thoughts had already flown to

Philip and what he would do now. "May we all go to Town? I do not think I can bear to wait here for news."

"Would it do any good if I said no?"

"I agree with Amelia," Meg replied. "I am not yet near my time, and London is but a short journey. We will only fret here, and you will wish to be where you can have news."

"Very well. I will meet you in Town. I will call in at the house on my way and direct Timmons to be prepared for your arrival."

Luke hurried away and Amelia joined Meg on the sofa. As soon as her sister's arm came around her, she burst into tears. Whether from worry for Philip or for being left behind, she could not say the cause, but she had held her feelings inside too long and they all came rushing out.

Philip sat atop Scipio and surveyed his land, from the lush, green valley to the rolling waters of the Thames. He had broken down in tears when he had first set foot on his Berkshire estate, which he had thought was lost to him forever. The last three weeks had been spent riding the grounds and meeting with his steward—Fielding had not only managed Philip's affairs during his absence, he had more than doubled the latter's estate and wealth. Philip could not believe it—he certainly did not deserve it.

Despite being engrossed in affairs on his estate, he could not help but think of Amelia and wish she were by his side. He deeply regretted not asking for her hand, because surely, he could not be more miserable than he was now, in his regrets of keeping quiet. It was an open wound of his own making, and the only hope of repair was her. Several times, he had stopped himself from riding off to Somerton, but he wanted to give her time to recover and decide what her true feelings were. Once she was in the bosom of what was familiar to her, she might long for one of those titled gentlemen possessed of wealth and position in Society.

Soon, he would return to his army duties. He expected a letter of summons any day now. Wellington would have returned to the Continent by now and would know of the destruction that had been wrought upon the fortress. There was little more to do here now, anyway; he had visited every one of his tenants and the grounds were in excellent condition. He took one last, longing look at his beautiful estate, then turned his horse towards London, to visit his sister for his remaining time on leave.

Somerton was on his way, and he decided to visit Amelia and follow his instincts once he was in her presence. Many times he had thought to write to Waverley to see how she did, but he had refrained, fearing that was a cowardly way to approach the situation. Urging Scipio on, he started his journey with great anticipation, for he could have Amelia in his arms within a few hours if all went well.

When he turned Scipio through the gates of Somerton, a few hours later, he was to be disappointed. A groom came out to take his horse as he rode into the stable yard.

"I'm afraid you just missed his Grace, Captain."

"Where was he headed?" Philip asked. He was not necessarily there to see Luke.

"He went off to London, sir. Hoping for news of army affairs," he said.

"Are her Grace and Lady Amelia at home?"

"You just missed them, too. They left an hour past, in the carriage, to join him in Town."

Philip wondered if he had missed an important dispatch. He would hurry onwards, himself.

"Thank you. Do you tend to my horse? I will go and attempt to charm Mrs. Bates out of some luncheon while Scipio rests. I will be ready for him in an hour."

"Yes, sir! I will give him a good rub down and then a feed of oats to fettle him." The groom led the horse off into a stall and Philip walked to the house in a state of concern. Things were happening faster than he had expected if, indeed, military matters were what had taken Waverley to Town.

Mrs. Bates placed him near the fire in the study and he warmed himself with tea and a hearty stew Cook had prepared for the servants. He finished the meal with satisfaction and went to Waverley's desk to avail himself of pen and paper, intending to leave a note for Lady Amelia. It would be forwarded to her in Town should he not have a chance to see her before he had to depart. He swallowed hard and prayed that would not be the case.

However, he spied an open letter in Tobin's handwriting on the top of the desk and he read its contents, knowing Waverley would not mind if it was left out in the open.

The urgency with which they had departed to London began to make sense, and he decided to wait before writing to Amelia, for he still had hope he would have time to speak with her.

Scipio was rested and ready for the task of the remaining miles from Richmond, and they reached London just as the sun was beginning to set. Like a lovesick swain, he did not wait to send a note and beg for an audience. Surely they were past that, after all they had been through together? They were good friends, if they could not be more, and he refused to let their meeting be awkward. So why was his stomach in knots and his hands shaking with fear?

A groom took his horse at the mews and Timmons opened the door before he could knock.

"Good evening, Captain Elliot. His Grace is in his study."

"Thank you, Timmons." Philip had meant to ask for Lady Amelia immediately, but it would perhaps be best to see what knowledge Luke had gained before offering anything to Amelia.

"Philip!" Luke said with a smile as the door opened, and came from behind his desk to offer a hearty handshake.

"I had not expected you. What a welcome surprise!"

"I stopped at Somerton, and was directed here. Forgive my intrusion, but I saw the letter from Tobin on your desk. Have you discovered anything else? I have not yet been to Headquarters."

"Unfortunately, yes." Waverley turned around and retrieved a paper from his desk and handed it to Philip. "I had news that some regiments are being sent back from America with all haste."

"I suspect that means my time here is short." He sighed heavily.

"Please take me with you," a voice pleaded from the doorway.

Philip spun about and his heart filled with joy at the sight of Lady Amelia.

"I will leave the two of you to...resolve matters between you," Waverley said, but Philip barely heard him. He was too busy opening his arms to gather Amelia to him.

"I have waited for this every moment since I last had you here," Philip said into her hair.

"Then why did you stay away so long?"

"I was putting my affairs in order, and I wanted to give you time to recover."

"You certainly did," she retorted and he laughed.

He pulled back to arm's length and looked down at her. "You are well, then?"

"In body... but my mind and soul have been in agony these past weeks. I do not ever want to be without you again."

"Nor I, you," he admitted without hesitation. "However, if there is another war, I can make no promises for the future. Following the drum is not an easy task."

"I am ready for it. There is nothing for me here without you."

"And if you are widowed shortly?"

"Then I shall be a widow who knew true love for a short time. I would rather that than nothing at all."

He looked her in the eye and saw reflected there an earnestness to match his own and pulled her back into his arms.

"You dear girl. You have made me very happy, though I realize I am being inordinately selfish."

"It is not selfishness if I want the same thing."

"No... but you do not yet realize the harsh realities of life with the army. We ride for long, hard hours, in harsh conditions, and often for many days at a time. Sometimes we have no food. Sometimes we sleep on the cold ground. You will see dead and wounded..."

"It is where I want to be—at your side. I know it will be far from easy, but it will be more fulfilling than yearning for you, and wasting away my days in a drawing room here."

"There will be no time for a grand London wedding, you know, if you mean to be Mrs. Elliot before I depart."

"I certainly do!" She looked offended that he had even considered her capable of desiring a fashionable ceremony.

"Then I will arrange a license while you organize the packing of your trunks." He gave her a quick kiss on the forehead and made to leave but she called him back.

"Philip? I will try to make you proud so you will never regret offering for me."

He took her face and cradled it in his hands. "I do not think it is possible to be more proud than I already am."

Feeling as though it was his first kiss, delicious sensations ran through his body as their lips touched. Her comforting scent of violets filled his senses and told him that this was what he had sought—he was home; she was the one. Amelia began to return the kiss with intensity and he could not wait to make her his own and lose himself in their love. She wound her hands around his neck and pulled him closer, into the magical intoxication of their affection.

He pulled back, putting his forehead to hers, and smiled.

"Thank you for not forgetting me."

EPILOGUE

*W*eddings and funerals were reliably good reunions, Philip reflected, one notably happier than the other. The last time they had all been together was the horrible day of Peter's death. Today, they gathered for the union of Philip to his bride, Lady Amelia. It was a somewhat rushed occasion, due to his anticipating a return to his army duties, and he was grateful all of his brethren could attend.

Saint George's was able to accommodate their small party, which was more than he would have expected. Luke, Matthias, James, Colin and Kitty were all present, Brethren through thick and thin. Adelaide was here, too, despite being heavy with child, walking on the arm of Major Fielding and looking happier than Philip ever could have hoped for.

Never would he have a guessed, almost a year ago now as he lay left for dead on a beach in France, that he would live to see this happy occasion.

Amelia appeared to be fully recovered from her injuries in France, and looked more beautiful than the first day he had seen her. Now, there were depths to her—scars of character—which only served to increase his attraction to her.

When Philip saw her standing at the back of the nave on Waverley's arm, he felt a rush of elation. It was as though God had made this woman especially for him and he was fortunate he had realized it. Philip could only hope he was worthy of her.

She was radiant, the smile on her face and the pink in her cheeks glowing as she glided down the aisle in a lavender gown that shimmered like the stars with every movement she made. Beyond those details, he saw only her face and the love in her eyes as Waverley handed her to him. The Reverend spoke and they recited their vows, but he did not hear as much as he should have done.

He could only be certain he had made the right choice, even though he knew it was a selfish one. There may not be much time left on Earth for him, being a soldier, but he would make sure he did not waste another moment.

Captain and Mrs. Elliot exited the church, this cold day in early March, to the cheers of the commoners who had gathered to watch. They entered the waiting carriage and tossed vails to the crowd before driving the short distance to Waverley Place to celebrate the wedding-breakfast with their friends and family.

"Well, Mrs. Elliot? Any regrets?" Amelia was so beautiful with the sun hitting her face through the window making her look like an angel. Could it be real that she was his?

"Only that you have not kissed me yet," she replied.

"That can be remedied this instant." He took her in his arms and found that the passion was only intensified the more you loved someone. Amelia tasted as sweet as he remembered, her mouth giving deliciously beneath his. Sliding his arms around her back, he held her close, curving her body gently over his arm as he deepened the kiss. A sigh escaped her and he boldly nibbled her lower lip. Her lips parted and his innocent beloved followed his lead to devastating effect. His body warmed all over, and a surprising flood of emotion came over him. He felt a warm tear drip onto his skin and was shocked to discover it was his. Pulling away from the kiss, he instead hugged her as close as he could, cherishing the faith she was putting in him by joining her life with his.

Neither of them noticed that the carriage had stopped. Someone opened the door and quickly shut it again. Philip and Amelia dissolved into laughter.

"I do believe you have compromised me, sir," Amelia teased.

"Then I fear you are forever shackled with me."

"It is good that I love you, then."

Philip released her, sat back, and took her beautiful face between his hands. Those bright blue eyes looked into his with such loyalty and devotion it astonished him. There was nothing more her wanted than to be the husband she deserved.

"I love you more than I ever thought it possible to love another being, Amelia."

"Oh, Philip." A sob escaped her throat and she kissed him again. All of the hope of a new beginning expressed in the simple action of melding lips, yet it was a yielding of self one to the other. It felt like anything was possible as he loved her with all his being.

Unfortunately, reality awaited outside.

"Shall we face our friends?"

"If we must."

"Yes, we must. It will be some time before we see them again."

Amelia looked a little sad at his words, but smiled. "I will miss them, but I would rather be with you."

"Thank you," he said dryly.

She rapped him on the arm and knocked on the carriage door. A footman opened it and handed her down before Philip could do so. He shook his head and climbed down, only to see his brethren standing before them, looking vastly amused.

"Do not say it." Philip held up his hands. "I have everything I deserve and more."

Waverley slapped him on the back. "I will refrain from comment, except to say better you than me."

"I will forgive you," James said, "but only because I could not afford her."

Kitty stepped forward and kissed him on the cheek. "I wish you every happiness, Philip." He wanted to know how she did, but it was not the right time to ask.

Matthias was next to offer his congratulations. "I never thought you would be the next to marry."

"You do seem to be shirking your familial responsibilities, Thackeray. Have you anyone in mind?"

"We will not speak of me on your special day, thank you."

The brethren all laughed.

"I suppose it is my turn to wish you well," Colin said, stepping forward. "However, I cannot feel easy about the situation in France. Waverley informed us of your activities since we last saw you."

"That must have taken some time," Philip retorted. "Lady Amelia knows precisely what she is getting herself into, I must say. It is selfish of me to ask it of her, but I confess I am honoured and privileged to have her by my side, come what may."

"Hear, hear," Waverley said. "I think we should toast to that indoors, where it is warm."

The six of them made their way into the dining room, where a feast lay waiting for them on the sideboard, and other friends and family were waiting to celebrate.

They ate and they danced, and Philip could not help but wonder if they would ever all be together like this again. Hours later, after the celebration had ended and the guests had left, Waverley found Philip before they all retired and handed him a packet.

"This came from Wellington, but I dared not give it to you before."

Philip gave him a knowing look as he accepted it and ran his finger under the familiar seal.

Captain,

YOU MAY HAVE HEARD *by now that I was posted to Vienna. I received news only moments ago that Napoleon has escaped Elba and is probably already back in France. It will be widely known soon. Please make haste to Brussels and join the contingent there. I am certain we will be grateful that their supplies are lessened when we face them across the field, as I fear we must and very soon. I will see you in Brussels, where your expertise on the matter of La Glacier and the Emperor's intentions will be greatly valued.*

WELLINGTON

PHILIP HANDED the paper to Waverley. "I am to join the contingent in Brussels immediately."

Amelia came in the room. "What has happened?"

"Napoleon has escaped."

She sank onto a nearby chair. "It is as we feared."

"Yes. I must depart for Brussels immediately."

Amelia nodded her head absently, but did not betray emotion or dissolve into tears.

"We cannot accompany you, with Meg so near to her confinement," Waverley said, a trace of regret in his voice.

"I would not ask it of you," Amelia answered. "But I intend to go. My husband will not be taken from me on this, my wedding day."

Philip would have expected no less. He smiled and drew her up into his arms as Waverley discreetly stepped from the room and closed the door.

"That's my girl," he whispered.

"I will not be forgotten," she said, as she pulled him down for another kiss.

"Impossible."

PREVIEW GENTLEMEN OF KNIGHTS SERIES

Duke of Knight

*R*owley Knight, Duke of Knighton, stood at the window of his study, hands clasped behind his back and stared out at the vast parkland which was largely concealed by the rain blowing sideways and striking the panes. He did not particularly notice the weather, for his mind was consumed with his responsibilities. It was a deuced nuisance, having four siblings, but he loved them in his own way—even if it was not a particularly affectionate one.

Lord Heath, the second eldest, was probably now stumbling in from his night's revelries in London. Rowley shook his head. Soon, he might have to intervene there, but he still had hopes that Heath would have sown his last wild oats – if he did not kill himself first.

Lord Edmund was the third sibling, and Rowley worried about him for other reasons. He was entirely too pious and tender-hearted for his own good. One day, Rowley hoped to lure him away from trying to save his parishioners in the London slums to a safer parish where he himself owned the living.

Then, there was Felix, who served on Wellington's staff, and even though Rowley worried about him, he knew Wellington kept an eye out for his welfare. If only Napoleon would cooperate.

His most pressing concern for the nonce, however, was his young sister, Eugenia. At sixteen years of age, she was turning into a young woman, and Rowley was at a loss as how to deal with her and the violent emotions that overtook her with no warning. After long deliberation, he had come to the decision to hire a companion-governess for her. Rowley did not want a new person, especially a woman, added to his household, but he could think of no other way—and he had tried.

If his calculations were correct, he had about half an hour left before the woman's arrival. Miss Lancaster had been thoroughly investigated and selected from several hundred women by Cummins, his man of business. None of those available from the various agencies had satisfied Cummins or Rowley, so he had found her upon the recommendation of his Aunt Violet, which was his only reservation. The girl was young and inexperienced; however, she was well educated and came from a good family which had fallen on hard times thanks to her father's gaming habits. While not opposed to charitable works, it was not his primary concern. Edmund fulfilled that role for the Knighton Duchy. Row's only care was the lady's suitability for Eugenia—and for staying out of his way.

The rain eased a little, and Rowley thought he detected the sounds of hooves on the gravel drive. He checked his pocket watch and noted with approval that at least the woman was timely. He could not abide tardiness.

Watching as the party alighted from the carriage, it was difficult to obtain a satisfactory glimpse as the footmen efficiently ushered everyone into the house under umbrellas. Reluctantly, Rowley tried to prepare himself for this necessary intrusion upon his sanctum. If all went well, Eugenia's entrée into womanhood would be guided by someone of the female sex and thus some measure of peace would return to his daily routine.

The expected knock on the door came shortly afterwards.

"Your guests have arrived, your Grace."

Rowley nodded and followed his butler, Banks, down the hall to the drawing room.

"Your Grace, may I present Lady Hambridge, Lady Sybil Mattingly, and Miss Lancaster."

Rowley withheld his groan. His aunt could never resist the chance to matchmake. He made polite bows to the guests, and kissed his aunt on the cheek.

"I trust your journey was comfortable?" Rowley asked, as he discreetly tried to see the new member of the household, but her bonnet was so large he could scarce see her face or her colouring, save one militant spark from her eyes.

He knew Lady Sybil's family and had little interest in the young girl just out of the schoolroom, who had not yet outgrown her spots or her childhood roundness.

"As comfortable as a long carriage ride can be," his aunt said as she sat down and waved the other two ladies to do the same. "It would help if you lived closer than Devon, but I suppose that cannot be helped."

Rowley did not bother to remark on the fact that the duchy and its holdings had been settled several hundred years before.

"Would you care for some refreshments before you are shown to your rooms?"

"Tea would be just the thing, Knighton."

Rowley glanced at Banks, who gave a nod and left the room. Rowley knew he would also direct the maids to prepare a room for the unexpected Lady Sybil, though truly, he did not know why he was surprised. This was not the first time his aunt had brought single ladies unannounced, in hopes of catching his attention. He refused to attend most events of the Season, so she brought ladies to him. It would make the business of arranging the post for Miss Lancaster more awkward, but so be it.

"If you do not object, your Grace, I think I should like to refresh myself, first," Miss Lancaster pronounced as she stood up.

Rowley and his aunt exchanged glances. "Of course," Rowley said, also rising, "I will have Mrs. Haynes show you to your room."

"I think I will join her," Lady Sybil said shyly.

When the ladies had gone, Rowley sat back down and leaned his head against the chair.

"We have only been here five minutes, Knighton. Are you already bored of us?"

He cast an elevated eyebrow at his aunt, and otherwise ignored the rhetorical question. "Does she know why she is here?"

"Unless she is a widgeon, she does. I told her Lady Eugenia was in need of female guidance."

Rowley scoffed. "And she is in need of funds and a home, but does she realize she will not be chaperoned and be required to earn her keep?"

"She will know soon enough, if she does not yet."

"And dare I ask why Lady Sybil is here?"

"Sybil is also my god-daughter and they are friends from school. I thought it would be pleasant for them to spend a few more days together."

"Very well. As long as you do not attempt any tricks with a mind to matrimony."

"Hush! The ladies will return at any moment," his aunt chastised.

"Then I will have Eugenia sent for. The sooner I can establish if they will make shift together, the sooner I can attempt to return to my duties."

"Duty, duty, duty!" She threw up her hands. "When will you stop concerning yourself with everyone else and look to your own future?"

"I have all the future I need," he snapped coldly. "I do not wish to repeat an argument you will not win, Aunt."

"Oh, very well." She tossed her hand, wafting a handkerchief in exasperation. "Do not say I did not try!" She looked heavenward, clearly affronted.

"No one can fault your efforts," he drawled, wishing this interview were at an end. He had no patience for feminine dramatics or wiles, and he sensed a guilt-ridden lecture was bound to follow. Banks entered with the tea tray and Rowley sent for Eugenia, anxious to avoid his aunt's tirade and to have all settled. He refused to listen to one more lecture on why he needed a wife. He did not have to.

***

"Why, Sybil, why him, of all people?" Emma asked as she frantically paced the room, tearing at the ribbons of her bonnet and tossing it on the bed.

"Did Lady Hambridge not tell you who you would be working for?" Lady Sybil asked with a wrinkled brow. She removed her own bonnet, then tidied her locks in front of the glass.

Emma shook her head. "I did not think to ask, either. How could I have been so stupid?"

"You were rather preoccupied," Lady Sybil suggested. "Maybe it will not be so bad. You will be spending most of your time with his sister, not him."

"Did you see the scowl on his face? And... and... how large he was?" she asked, her eyes wide with dismay.

"He is just reserved—and he is not so very big. You came to his shoulders." Lady Sybil pointed to her own shoulder to indicate, as if it was the same thing.

"No, I cannot do this. He frightens me. His eyes…"

"I think him rather handsome; and he is a duke, which makes up for a great deal."

"You may have him!" Emma retorted. "Wait—you stay here with me and woo the duke, and I may hide in the schoolroom with his sister."

"I would if I could, dearest Emma. I will be remaining a few days, at any rate, so you may form a better opinion whilst his aunt and I are here. Besides, they gave you a lovely room, which means they intend to treat you better than a servant."

Emma bit her lower lip as she looked around at the beautiful white and pale blue room, decorated more finely than hers had been before...the money was all gone. "I suppose so."

"Take a deep breath and let us go back down for tea. Everything is better after tea."

Emma allowed herself to be ushered back down to the drawing room. She did not know how she was going to bear this. Her nature was neither meek nor subservient, and she had witnessed the Duke's dictatorial, haughty manner before. Would he remember her? It was improbable, but her feelings towards him were tainted; equally, it was unlikely she would find another post as lucrative as this. Swallowing her pride, she held her head high as she entered the drawing room. She would have to force herself to bite her tongue and avoid the Duke as much as possible.

"Oh, you have returned," Lady Hambridge said as the Duke rose to his feet.

"I trust everything was satisfactory with your chamber?" he asked, clearly assessing her.

Please do not let him remember me. Please do not let him remember me.

"Yes, your Grace." She remembered to curtsy just in time.

"Excellent. May I present to you my sister, Lady Eugenia?"

"I am pleased to make your acquaintance, my lady." She curtsied.

"Miss Lancaster will be your new companion and governess, Genie."

"Oh! How exciting! I have never had a female companion before, except for Nurse, and she does not count since she is more than twice my age. Did you know I have four brothers and not one sister?" she asked Emma.

"I did not. I was blessed with a sister. It will be a pleasure to be your companion."

"Thank you, Rowley! What a wonderful surprise, to be sure!" the girl exclaimed.

Everyone sat down, and Emma could feel the Duke's eyes upon her. It was all she could do not to squirm under his scrutiny and glare back at him. Instead, she focused her gaze on her new charge. Lady Eugenia was a gangly youth, just coming into her womanhood, with bright blue eyes and silky black curls. She was lively, and full of questions for Lady Hambridge and Lady Sybil. Emma used the opportunity to study and observe, but so did the Duke. He said little and stared, and she could not ignore him, although she tried. His presence filled the room like a thick smoke that permeated all of a person's senses—suffocating them. Could he not leave and let her become acquainted with Eugenia?

"Miss Lancaster, may I have a few moments of your time?"

Emma looked up in surprise.

"To discuss the particulars?" he prompted.

"Yes, of course." Emma's heart began to race as she followed him into a study. What was there to discuss? She knew she would be paid two hundred pounds per annum, plus a clothing allowance for attending *ton* events when chaperoning Lady Eugenia.

The room was smaller and she felt confined. His presence was stronger in here, if that were possible, and she longed to escape or thrust her head out of the window for some fresh air.

"Do you think you will be content here?" he asked, disturbing her thoughts. He had not said happy, but content, she noticed.

"I shall try, your Grace," she replied, endeavouring to avoid making eye contact with him. He saw too much. "Your sister seems a very pleasant girl. I think we shall deal quite well together."

"I am glad to hear it. Nothing is more important to me than my family."

Emma could not resist meeting his eyes, then. She knew all about how he dealt with people who crossed him and his beloved family. She looked away before he saw the hatred in her eyes and dismissed her on the spot.

"Of course, your Grace," she muttered in a forced voice. She would have to control her emotions better than this. If only she had known and could have prepared herself.

"And the pay is satisfactory?"

"It is very generous, your Grace."

An awkward silence followed before he finally spoke again. "Miss Lancaster, I am a man of few words and prefer my own company for the most part. However, if you ever need anything, do not hesitate to ask."

"Thank you, your Grace." Emma stood to leave, assuming this uncomfortable interview was at an end.

"There is one more thing. Do I know you from somewhere?"

AFTERWORD

Author's note: British spellings and grammar have been used in an effort to reflect what would have been done in the time period in which the novels are set. While I realize all words may not be exact, I hope you can appreciate the differences and effort made to be historically accurate while attempting to retain readability for the modern audience.

Thank you for reading *Not Forgotten.* I hope you enjoyed it. If you did, please help other readers find this book:

1. This ebook is lendable, so send it to a friend who you think might like it so she or he can discover me, too.
2. Help other people find this book by writing a review.
3. Sign up for my new releases at www.Elizabethjohnsauthor.com, so you can find out about the next book as soon as it's available.
4. Connect with me at any of these places:

www.Elizabethjohnsauthor.com
Facebook

Instagram
Amazon
Bookbub
Goodreads
elizabethjohnsauthor@gmail.com

ACKNOWLEDGMENTS

There are many, many people who have contributed to making my books possible.

My family, who deals with the idiosyncrasies of a writer's life that do not fit into a 9 to 5 work day.

Dad, who reads every single version before and after anyone else—that alone qualifies him for sainthood.

Wilette and Anj, who take my visions and interprets them, making them into works of art people open in the first place.

My team of friends who care about my stories enough to help me shape them before everyone else sees them.

Heather who helps me say what I mean to!

And to the readers who make all of this possible.
I am forever grateful to you all.

ALSO BY ELIZABETH JOHNS

Surrender the Past

Seasons of Change

Seeking Redemption

Shadows of Doubt

Second Dance

Through the Fire

Melting the Ice

With the Wind

Out of the Darkness

After the Rain

Ray of Light

Moon and Stars

First Impressions

The Governess

On My Honour